KILLERS ON
A HOLDUP SPREE

Morgan heard spurs jingle as the two men crossed the front of the bank. Both held guns, but it was the older of the two who gave orders.

"Put the money in the sack," he said. When the banker didn't move, old man Hall fired a shot at his feet. "It's up to you how you die," he said. "Slow, or do I put a slug in your brisket?"

Morgan shoved the door open enough to step through. "Hook the moon, Hall," he barked.

For a second neither man moved. Then they both wheeled, firing. The room roared with the sound of three men swapping lead.

NIGHTMARE IN BROKEN BOW

by
Wayne D. Overholser

A DELL BOOK

Published by
Dell Publishing Co., Inc.
1 Dag Hammarskjold Plaza
New York, New York 10017

Dell ® TM 681510, Dell Publishing Co., Inc.

ISBN: 0-440-16418-4

Printed in the United States of America
First printing—January 1980

NIGHTMARE
IN
BROKEN BOW

CHAPTER I

The beat of hoofs was coming closer and closer; he felt the familiar, belly-freezing grip of fear. He was paralyzed. He could not move. He knew they were coming to kill him.

Mark Morgan sat up in bed, his body covered with sweat, the paralysis of fear continuing to grip him. He didn't know how many times he'd had this nightmare. There were several variations to it, but basically it was always the same: the steady hammer of hoofs on the frozen ground that kept coming closer and closer and louder and louder, and yet for some strange reason he always woke up before the riders arrived.

He rubbed his face with his hands, the palms wet with sweat. He forced his feet to the floor and sat on the edge of the bed, trembling. It always took him several minutes to recover from the nightmare, and it was that way this morning.

Aunt Kate's Dominique rooster welcomed the morning with his lusty crow from the chicken pen in the backyard. It was full daylight. Mark guessed it was about six. Aunt Kate always got up at half past six to start breakfast, but he didn't hear her in the kitchen, so he knew it was not that late.

He rubbed his face with his hands again, knowing there was no use trying to go back to sleep. He dressed, the old nerve-wracking question nagging him again. Was the nightmare based on fact, or was it only what it seemed to be, a nightmare? Had something really happened when he was a child that kept triggering the nightmare? He was twenty-three years old; he had asked Aunt Kate that question many times, but she never really answered it for him.

He buckled his gun belt around him, picked up his hat from where he had laid it on the bureau, and rubbed a sleeve across the deputy's star on his vest. He was proud of the star which he had worn for more than a year, and because he was proud, he liked to keep it shiny bright. Childish, he told himself, but to him the star was a symbol, and he could not bear to see it dulled by blurred, sweaty fingerprints.

As he left his bedroom and crossed the front room to the door, Aunt Kate called, "I'll start breakfast right away, Mark."

"Don't bother," he said. "I'll eat at the Bon Ton."

He realized, too late, that he had snapped at her. He felt guilty because he cared about her. She had raised him; they had come to Springfield when he was three. He had many memories of his childhood life here; he remembered nothing about his life before that, but he had an intuitive feeling that the terrifying nightmares which kept returning night after night were based on something that had happened before he'd come to Springfield, something so terrifying that it had blotted out every event that had happened during the first three years of his life.

Now, walking toward the business block, the warm June sun falling upon the prairie and throwing his long shadow beside him, he knew he could not stay here and continue to be plagued by these nightmares. He was born in Converse County in the northern part of the state near the Wyoming line. He would never be free of the nightmares until he returned and found out what had happened during those first three years.

Aunt Kate would be unhappy when he left, but she had a good job keeping house for Major Bert Rancey, a Civil War veteran who had lost his wife a year ago. She would probably sell the house where she lived now and move in with the major. He might even marry her in time if Mark wasn't here for her to look after.

No, she'd be all right. As long as he could remember, back to that evening long ago when they had stepped down from the stage here in Springfield, she had lived for him. She was in her early forties, far from an old woman. It was time she started living for herself. He should have left before this, he thought, but every time he had mentioned it, she cried and carried on as if he was breaking her heart.

The Bon Ton was open. He stepped in and called, "Good morning," to Cherry Lynn, the waitress. She smiled, dimples appearing briefly in her cheeks. "Good morning to you, Deputy," she said. "What's the matter with your Aunt Kate? Wouldn't she get out of bed this morning."

"She was up," Mark said. "I just got to thinking about your scrambled eggs and ham and biscuits, and I knew I had to have some this morning."

Cherry giggled. "You're as full of blarney as ever.

9

Your Aunt Kate is a better cook than I am." She waggled a finger at him. "I know what you're up to, but it won't work with me. I'm not hypnotized by your handsome face like most girls around here."

"Go on," he said. "Get my breakfast."

She giggled again and disappeared into the kitchen. As always she encouraged him while pretending not to. He knew she was as willing as the next girl, and he was irritated by the lengths some of them would go just to acquire a husband. He was a good catch, he supposed, now that he had been appointed deputy and Sheriff Abe Gilroy had announced he would not run again and that he expected Mark to take his place next year.

Cherry brought his eggs and ham, a plate of biscuits, and a cup of coffee, then fluttered back and forth behind the counter trying to talk, but he was in no mood for it. He finished eating, paid, and slid off the stool.

"You coming to the dance Saturday night?" Cherry asked hopefully.

She fluttered her eyelids at him, as frank an invitation as a woman could give a man. He paused, one hand on the doorknob, and looked back over his shoulder at her. He could do worse, he told himself, if he were looking for a wife.

"I won't be here," he said.

The hopeful smile left her lips. "Where are you going?" she asked.

"I don't know for sure," he said and stepped out into the June sunshine.

He strode on toward the courthouse, uneasy now that he had to face Sheriff Gilroy and tell him he was leaving. Funny thing, he thought, how he had finally made up his mind to leave. Nothing had happened that was significant. It was just the cumulative pressure of the nightmares which made waiting intolerable, but he didn't think anyone would understand that.

He found the sheriff in his office as he had expected even at this early hour. Gilroy was an old man so stove up by rheumatism that he could not stay in bed more than a few hours at a time, so he spent his days and parts of the nights here in his office, dozing in his swivel chair or walking around the courthouse gossiping with the other county officials.

"Well now," Gilroy said, leaning back in his chair, "what brings you out so early? We ain't chasing no outlaws today."

Mark took his star off and laid it on the desk. "I'm resigning, Abe," he said. "I've got to get out of Baca County."

"The nightmare again?" Gilroy asked.

Mark nodded. "I'll never get rid of them as long as I don't know what happened when I was little, and I'll never find out staying here."

"I ain't surprised about your leaving," the sheriff said, "but damn it, I can't run this office without you. I've been training you to take my place ever since you first pinned on the star. You're a good lawman, Mark, the best deputy I ever had. Now where will I find a man to replace you?"

"I don't rightly know," Mark said. "All I know is that I've got to go back to Converse County."

Gilroy tapped his fingertips on the desk, frowning, then he said, "All right. I sure won't try to talk you out of it, seeing as I can't anyway, with your mind made up the way it is. You want a deputy job when you get to Converse County?"

"What makes you think I could get one?"

"I ain't sure you can," Gilroy said, "but I had a letter awhile back from the sheriff up there saying he needed a deputy and did I know of a good man who would work for one hundred dollars a month. Maybe he's found one by now, but it ain't likely, seeing as Converse County is a graveyard for deputies. Three have been gunned down up there in the last six months. I'd hate to see you take the job if it's still open, but I reckon you'll have to find something to do and being deputy will beat punching cows."

"It would for a fact," Mark said, "and I'd have a better chance digging into what happened twenty years ago if I was a deputy."

"I'll write a letter for you," Gilroy said. "I know Al Burke. I had to go up there a year or so ago to fetch back a prisoner. Burke's a few years older'n you, about thirty, I'd guess. He's had the job ever since he was twenty-one years old. He's a queer one. He likes to say he's a coward and lazy as a fat pup, but he ain't neither one."

Gilroy took paper, pen, and ink from his desk drawer, wrote a short letter, and showed it to Mark. He merely said that Mark had served under him as deputy with distinction and could be depended on to do his duty. Mark nodded, said, "Thanks," and, folding the sheet of paper, slipped it into his shirt pocket.

"I didn't want to blow your horn too loud," Gilroy said. "It's my guess Burke won't want too good a man, and that may be your trouble. Him and his family run the County. There's some lawlessness up there they seem to wink at. I dunno why he's lost three deputies unless they were just incompetent.

"Like I said, I'd rather keep you here. I don't much cotton to the notion of you being deputy under Burke, but damn it, just stay alive for a couple of months and after you find out what you want to know, come back to Baca County and go to work for me again."

"I aim to stay alive," Mark said, extending his hand. "Thanks for . . ." He stopped, suddenly aware that Gilroy had done a great deal for him and he had never said a word of thanks to the old man. "Hell, Abe, I can't begin to thank you. You know that."

Gilroy said, "No thanks necessary," and shook his hand. "One thing, though. What made you decide this so sudden like?"

"I don't know," Mark said. "I woke up again this morning, sweating and shaking and scared, and I decided I had to free myself from the nightmares. I'll have 'em the rest of my life if I don't do it."

Gilroy nodded. "I'd do the same, I reckon. I'll miss you, son."

"I'll be back," Mark said and left the courthouse.

CHAPTER II

When Mark returned to the house, Aunt Kate was in the kitchen. He had intended to go directly into his bedroom, pick up his gear, and make his good-bye as brief as possible, but when she called to him, he sensed an urgency in her voice that he could not disregard.

He crossed the living room and went on into the kitchen. Aunt Kate had poured a cup of coffee for him. She motioned for him to sit down, then turned back to the stove and replaced the coffeepot.

"How was Cherry?" she asked.

"Fine," he answered. "She's available."

Aunt Kate sniffed. "She always has been. You can do better."

She stood motionless, looking at him, a tall, raw-boned woman who appeared older than she was. She had a formidable look about her as if she were capable of handling any problem that came to her, a look that made some people afraid of her; but she had a great capacity for love and she had showered Mark with it.

He sipped his coffee, the silence oppressive, then she said, "You look naked without your star."

"I feel naked," he said.

"The sheriff will miss you," she said.

He nodded. "He told me he would."

"Why did you quit?"

He set his cup back on the table. He hesitated, not knowing how to say what he had to say, then he blurted, "I just can't stand the nightmares any more. I've had 'em since I was little. You know that. You remember how I'd wake up screaming when I was a little boy and you'd come and hold me and tell me I was all right. Well, I'm not all right. I never will be until I find out what happened."

"You've lived with your nightmares all this time," she said. "What made you decide you couldn't live with them any longer?"

"I don't know," he said. "It's like having a gallon can full of water. You keep putting a little more in until the water gets to the top, then the next spoonful you pour in runs over. I felt that way this morning. I'm sorry, Aunt Kate, but I've got to go."

She nodded. "I knew this was going to happen sooner or later, but I hate to see it come. You plan to come back here?"

"I figure on it," he said. "Abe said he'd have a job for me if I get back in a couple of months."

She came to the table and sat down across from him. "Tell me about the one you had last night."

"You've heard all of them," he said impatiently. "No sense repeating it."

"I want to hear it," she said, "and then I'll tell you what happened. Maybe I should have told you a long time ago, but when you were little, I thought being reminded of what had happened would make you more nervous than ever, and when you got older, I was afraid it would make you want to go back to get revenge."

He stared at her a long moment, not sure she would tell him everything he wanted to know, then he shrugged and decided he'd better find out as much as he could. He told her about the nightmare, and she nodded as if it was indeed familiar to her.

"Sometimes they are different, ain't they?" she asked.

"Yeah, some are longer," he said. "Sometimes there is a man on a horse who says, 'Hand the boy up to me.' He's always in a hurry. Then sometimes we're riding as hard as we can, but the hoofbeats are always behind us, and the man says, 'Take the boy, Kate. You can make it to the railroad.'"

"Yes," she said softly, "that's the way it was. Funny that a three-year-old boy would remember so much."

"I don't remember," he said sharply. "That's the hell of it. I should remember a few other things before we came here. Like having a dog. Or the house we lived in. Or what my father looked like." He shook his head. "It's all blank. It's as if this running and being chased was the beginning of my life, but you tell me I was three years old. A lot of things must have happened before that."

"Yes, there were," she agreed. "The house was made of stone with a big fireplace in the front room. You used to sit on your father's lap in front of that fireplace, and he'd tell you stories he'd made up. I used to get after him because some of them were horrible. About hungry bears and fierce mountain lions, but he'd laugh and say it was good for you to know about things like that."

He shook his head. "I don't remember any of that."

"Do you remember falling out of your high chair and getting a cut on your head and bleeding something fierce? We got you patched up and your pa said he'd buy you something when he went to town that afternoon. He brought you a big glass marble with some pretty geegaws inside."

"I don't remember," he said.

She sighed. "All right, I'll tell you what happened, and maybe it'll clear up your memory. Your father's name was Flint Cardigan. He had a brother Ed. I gave you my name when we came here. Morgan was your mother's maiden name.

"Your folks and Ed moved to Converse County before it was a county. They were about the first to settle in what they called East Park. There wasn't even a town then. Just a wilderness. They had to go to Laramie for supplies. They brought in a small herd of cattle and did well. It's high, about nine thousand feet, so the climate is terrible. Like they say, it's hell on women and horses.

"Your mother was young and purty when Flint married her. She died in childbirth and Flint sent for me. I went up there and kept house for them for three years.

"It had been just fine at first, then the Burkes moved in. They built the town of Broken Bow. They were responsible for making Converse County, and they had enough money to buy almost anything they wanted. During the three years I was there, they bought out most of the other ranches that they wanted, all but your pa's and Ed's.

"The trouble was Flint and Ed were the most stubborn men I ever seen. They wouldn't sell. The Burkes had brought in some gunmen, and Flint and Ed had a couple of gunfights and killed the Burke men. After that the Burkes decided to finish it off, so one night in town they jumped Flint and killed him.

"Ed got out of town and outran them. When he reached the ranch, we could hear them coming. There must have been a dozen or more. Jess Burke was the one who did the ranching. He must have had the whole Bar B crew with him. Ed said there wasn't much time, and I was to grab a few things and get you dressed while he saddled my horse. He gave me a little tin box that he said held all the money they had. He mounted and told me to hand you up to him just like it is in your nightmare, then we rode.

"I never rode so hard in my life. Once we looked back and saw a red light against the sky, so we knew they had fired the house. It didn't slow them up much, but maybe it was enough to let us get away. They kept gaining on us, and Ed said for me to take you and go on into town. We were to catch the train that morning. I took you and rode on, but before we got to town, I heard gunfire. I guess they caught Ed and killed him. I never heard, but I never saw him again."

She stopped and wiped her eyes. Mark, watching her, sensed how painful it had been to go over this. After a long silence she said, "Ed would have come here for me if he had got away. You see, we were in love and we were going to get married."

Maybe that was the reason she had never married after she had come here to Baca County. He thought about what she had said, aware that it fitted his nightmares. It was strange that his mind had held just a few fragments of what had happened that terrible night. He had not been old enough to realize how great the danger had been, but he must have sensed it from Kate's fear. All he knew now was that his memory of the first three years of his life was a complete blank.

"You think they would have killed us if they had caught us?" he asked.

"Oh, yes," she said. "You were the heir to the Cardigan ranch. That was what they wanted. By now it has been sold for taxes, and I'm sure the Burkes own it. There were two other Burke men besides Jess. Rodney was the oldest. He was the banker. Bob was the middle one. He ran the store.

"Together, you see, they could control everything in Converse County. It's a Burke empire. I haven't been back, of course, but I read about them in the newspaper. Now Jess's son Allan is the sheriff; so you see even the law, for whatever it amounts to, is Burke law. You'll just run into trouble if you go back and try to get even for what happened to your father and your uncle Ed."

She took a long breath and leaned across the table toward him. "Vengeance is the Lord's. Leave it to Him. I couldn't bear for you to be killed. That's why I never told you what happened. I knew you'd want to go back."

"I'm not going back to get revenge," he said. "I guess I just want to see what the country looks like and to see the Burkes. Maybe I won't stay." He rose. "You go ahead and sell this house and move into the major's place. He wants you. He'll take care of you."

He went into his bedroom and returned a moment later with his bedroll. Aunt Kate was still at the table. He bent down and kissed her.

"I know how much I owe you," he said. "I'm grateful. You've been all a mother could have been to me, but I can't stay here any longer."

When he left the kitchen, she was still sitting at the table. She did not turn to have one final look at him. As he opened the door and stepped outside, he heard her crying. He saddled his horse and rode north. He had no logical reason to doubt her story, but he could not keep from wondering if she had told him the whole truth.

CHAPTER III

Mark topped Aspen Pass near noon on the following Monday. He reined his sorrel up to let him blow, his gaze sweeping East Park, which stretched out below him like a giant bowl. The rim on the east and west was made up of snow-capped peaks. To the north a series of pine-clad ridges formed an undulating black line against the deep blue sky. The south rim would be exactly the same as the north, he thought, if he were there looking at it as he was looking at the north rim.

Long ridges covered by pine and spruce knifed into the park from the east and west sides, and here and there patches of quaking aspens made light green islands in the somber gray of the sagebrush that covered most of the park. He was surprised that the floor of the valley was not as flat as he had pictured it but was made up of a series of low, gently sloping ridges. Atop one of them far to the north was a collection of buildings that would be the town of Broken Bow.

He rode down the slope, winding back and forth between walls of close growing spruce trees, and soon came to a small stream that made a white-laced ribbon all the way to the base of the mountain. There it slowed to become a slow-moving, meandering creek flowing between willow-lined banks. It should be a perfect trout stream, he thought. Trout fishing was a sport he had never experienced in Baca County, and he looked forward to trying it here.

From here on the road made an almost direct line north to Broken Bow. He reached the town late in the afternoon, the long, grotesque shadow that he and his sorrel made flowing over the grass and sagebrush to his right. East Park would be, just as Aunt Kate had told him, fine cattle country, but as she had said, it would be hell on horses and women. The winters, he judged, would be incredibly severe.

From what Mark had seen that afternoon, it was plain that the park was not overgrazed. The few steers he had seen were in excellent condition. All were under the Bar B iron. He remembered Aunt Kate telling him that it was the Burke brand.

If the Burkes controlled Converse County as completely as Aunt Kate had said, they could protect it from being overgrazed, a calamity that had ruined many a northern range after the big herds had been trailed north from Texas.

The afternoon had been one of surprises. First, the park was far bigger than he had expected. It was a beautiful piece of country, completely opposite to the somber gray of the plains that he had grown up with in Baca County. That was on the plus side, but the town of Broken Bow was completely on the minus side.

As he rode down the deserted Main Street, it struck

Mark that he had never seen an uglier, more run-down town in his life than Broken Bow. Half of the buildings that fronted on Main Street were empty, their doors and windows boarded up. The buildings that were in use were weather-stained and needed painting. There was not a brick or stone building on Main Street, and nowhere was there a semblance of civic pride.

Ahead of him a gaunt, two-story building stood directly in his path. The street split and went on both sides of the building, then came together to form a county road that ran arrow-straight beyond the town until it was lost in the dusty distance. This would be the courthouse, he thought. Reaching it, he dismounted and tied at the hitch pole in front. He wondered if Al Burke would be in the sheriff's office this late in the afternoon.

He walked across the weed-covered yard to the front door. There was no hint of a grass lawn; there were no trees in the block that contained the courthouse. In fact, there wasn't a tree anywhere in town that he could see.

At the moment the air was still and warm, but the wind must blow across the park much of the time with galelike force, and there was nothing to stop it except this tawdry collection of frame and log buildings.

He climbed the steps, opened the door, and went into a dark hall. The county clerk's office was on one side, the county treasurer's on the other. At the far end of the hall he found the sheriff's office. He tried the door, but as he expected, it was locked.

He heard someone above him. Remembering that he had seen stairs near the front door, he retraced his steps along the hall and climbed the stairs. He found an old man sweeping the floor. At least Mark assumed he was sweeping. He was going through the motions, but judging from the amount of energy expended in the listless strokes of the broom, he wasn't moving much dirt.

The janitor stopped and leaned on his broom handle. "Looking for somebody, mister?" he asked, happy to have an excuse to stop working.

"I'm looking for Sheriff Burke."

"Oh, Al ain't never around on Mondays," the old man said. "He'll be back some time tomorrow."

"That means he's gone most of Tuesday, too," Mark said.

The janitor cackled. "That's a right smart observation, young feller. You're dead right. If we ever had a bad crime on Monday or Tuesday, I don't know what we'd do."

"Doesn't he have any deputies?"

"Deputies?" The janitor pursed his lips and spat in the direction of the spittoon. "No sir, he don't. They get killed as fast as he appoints 'em."

"Don't he pay enough to get good men?"

"Sure he does," the old man answered. "The county authorized one hundred dollars a month and in this county that makes a man rich. In the last six months three men, all gunslingers I'd say from their records, have been smoked down right here on the streets of Broken Bow."

"Who does it?"

The janitor shrugged. "Fur as evidence goes, nobody knows, but it's probably some of the Hall gang. You can count on that. Some of 'em like the Dorn boys ride into town once a month, or oftener if they hear Al's got a deputy. They raise hell in one way or another, and the deputy winds up dead. Always happens at night. Gets plugged as he walks along the street. Happens on Monday when Al's out of town."

"What is this Hall gang?"

"You ain't never heard of 'em?" the old man asked, surprised.

"Don't think so."

"Well, they ain't no Jesse James or Dalton gang fur as the general public goes, but around here they're a hell of a lot worse. There's three boys and their dad in the Hall family. They've got a little spread in the north end of the county in some mighty rough country, but they don't make no living out of it. The talk is they rob a bank up in Wyoming and then ride hell-for-leather back home. The Wyoming posse never catches 'em, and Al, he don't have no evidence they're the ones, so they never get nailed. Then there's others who live on the North Fork like the Dorn boys. I figure they're all in cahoots."

"How does it happen the deputies are the ones who get shot, not the sheriff?"

The janitor grinned, shifted his quid to the other side of his mouth, and shot another brown stream at the spittoon. He said, "I dunno about that. You can figure it out any way you want to. Folks around here do a lot of figuring, but they don't talk about it much. Of course everybody's got an explanation except the ones named Burke."

He wiped a hand across his mouth. "Hell, here I am running on like an old woman. I don't know nothing, you understand, but if you're fixing to live here, you'll learn a lot about the Halls and the Burkes. I don't reckon you'll talk much about it, either."

"Where does the sheriff go when he's out of town?"

"Dunno." The old man started to sweep again. "I've talked too damned much already. I figured maybe you was just riding through, but now I get a notion you're figuring on jumping Al about a deputy's job, so I knowed I'd gabbed too much. You tell Al what I said, and I'd lose my job. I'm too stove up to ride for the Bar B any more. They retired me to this job, and if I lose it, I reckon I'll just starve to death."

"Don't worry about me talking," Mark said, "but you're right about me seeing the sheriff about the deputy's job. I'm sorry I missed him."

The janitor straightened and leaned on his broom again, his gaze moving down Mark's tall body from the crown of his Stetson to the toes of his scuffed boots. "You look like you'll do, mister. If you want the job after what I've told you . . . Al, he'll tell you the same thing . . . I figure you'll get it; but I'd sure let somebody in town know the names and addresses of your next to kin. Doc Jones, he's the coroner, under-taker, and medico all rolled into one. He ought to know where to ship the body."

"You're a cheerful bastard," Mark said sourly and, wheeling, walked away.

He glanced back at the janitor just before he disap-peared down the stairs. The old man was still leaning on his broom, a glum expression on his stubble-covered face. As Mark crossed the front of the lot to his horse, he told himself that what the janitor had said jibed with what Sheriff Abe Gilroy had told him. He had a weird feeling that Broken Bow was very close to being a ghost town, that the crimes the Burkes had committed—the conniving and robbing and killing —were about to catch up with them.

He wondered if he was destiny's tool who would bring it about. It would be belated justice if that turned out to be the case.

CHAPTER IV

Mark left his horse in the livery stable, turning him over to a white-haired man who came toward him along the runway from the corral behind the stable. Mark told him he'd be staying in town for a few days at least, but tonight he wanted his horse rubbed down and given a double bait of oats. The old man shifted the unlighted cigar to the other side of his mouth, nodded, and didn't say a word.

Mark stepped back into the street carrying his blanket roll. He found the hotel in the middle of the block, a two-story building that was as weathered as its neighbors. The lobby held the usual desk and register along with two battered black couches, four captain's chairs, and a yellow-leafed geranium in the window that was struggling valiantly to stay alive.

No one was in sight. Mark banged the bell briskly three times before an old man with a white goat beard came from somewhere in the back of the building. Mark thought the town's population must be composed entirely of old men.

"I want a room," Mark said.

"I can sure give you one." The clerk stepped behind

the desk and shoved the register in Mark's direction. "Fact is, I've got two. Which one do you want?"

"Now how the hell would I know?" Mark demanded. "What's the difference in them?"

"None."

Mark signed his name and home address as Springfield, Colorado, thinking the old man was either off his rocker or had a very peculiar sense of humor. "What are the numbers?"

"Numbers one and two."

"I'll take one."

The clerk nodded as he studied Mark's signature and address. "Good. Number one is a fine room. Looks right down on the street. So you're from Springfield. That's a right smart ways from here."

"It is for a fact," Mark said. "Is there an eating place in town?"

The clerk pointed across the street. "Yes, sir. Sharon's Beanery it's called. Mighty good for a town like this."

"No key?"

The old man shook his head. "No key. Nobody steals anything in this town. Nothing to steal when you get right down to cases. Oh, I guess Rodney Burke has a little dinero in his safe, and Bob, he's the one who runs the store, has got a few things that might be worth a man's while, but that's about all."

Mark climbed the stairs, thinking that Broken Bow was even worse than it looked. If the hotel had only two rooms that were kept open, its business wasn't much to brag about. The clerk hadn't said they only kept two rooms open, but it was a reasonable assumption because Mark noticed that no one had signed the register for more than two weeks. Well, he'd look at the room and maybe decide to sleep in the sagebrush.

Surprisingly the room was clean. He checked the bedding and found that it was clean. So was the white pitcher and basin on the bureau. The room, he told himself, was the first good thing he'd found in Broken Bow.

He tossed his blanket roll on the bed, took off his shirt, and washed. Even the towel on the wall beside the bureau was clean. He dried, emptied the basin into the slop jar, and put his shirt on, thinking that Springfield was not much of a city, but compared to Broken Bow, it was a true metropolitan center.

He went down the stairs and crossed the lobby to the street, then stood there a moment, his eyes searching for Sharon's Beanery. It was not directly across the street as the clerk had pointed but was at the far end of the block, a small, one-story building with a new, black-lettered sign above the door, SHARON'S BEANERY. It was about the only evidence along Main Street that there was a can of paint anywhere in town.

Mark angled across the dust strip to the restaurant. As he opened the door, a cowbell hanging above it jangled loudly. He closed the door, relieved to find that the smell was appetizing. He also noticed that a healthy-looking geranium in the window held six brilliant red blossoms. There were now to his knowledge two good things in Broken Bow.

He'd had a depressing feeling that everything in Broken Bow was old and dying, but this geranium broke the pattern. He expected to see Sharon hobbling out of the kitchen, a woman as old as the men he had talked to, but the pattern was completely demolished when a girl appeared, a tall and very pretty girl who moved with unconscious grace. She was blond and blue eyed, with a smile that wiped out the sour mood that had been building in him.

"What will you have?" she asked, stopping across the counter from him. "I can't give you much choice. It will have to be ham or a steak."

"First I just want to look at you," he said. "You're like a breath of fresh air. I've never been in a town that got me down like this one. Nothing but weathered buildings and old men. Even the geranium in the hotel lobby looks like it's dying. Now you turn up as bright and pretty as a new red-wheeled buggy. You don't belong in Broken Bow."

She stared at him a moment, then she nodded, the smile fading. "You're right, mister. I don't belong here, and if I ever save enough money to get out of town, I'll be on my way, but that day isn't even close."

She motioned toward the hotel. "I feel sorry for that geranium. Old Bill forgets to water it, so I suppose it'll die and I'll root another one for him and it will die. It's depressing. If I didn't escape for an hour or two every day and get on a horse and ride, I'd die, too."

"I believe it," Mark said. "How about letting me ride with you tomorrow?"

She was startled. "You're a bold man for a stranger." She shook her head. "I'm sorry. I always ride alone."

"You can break the rule," he said.

She shook her head again. "I'm tempted, but I know you're joshing me. Now then, what will you have?"

"A steak."

"How do you like it?"

"Oh, just wave it across the frying pan a few times."

She disappeared into the kitchen. A moment later

31

he heard the sound of frying meat. He rolled a smoke and fired it, thinking that finding a girl like this was the same as waking up to a day that was clear and warm after a week of slow drizzle. He was curious about who she was and why she remained in Broken Bow. He guessed she was about twenty. Few girls attained that age without getting married in a country like this where there was always a scarcity of women.

She returned with a steak that more than covered the plate, a side dish of beans, a jar of honey, and a batch of hot biscuits. He started to eat at once, more hungry than he had realized. He paused long enough to say, "This sure beats prairie fare."

"You've come a ways?"

"From Springfield."

"Oh, that is a long ways." She studied him for a full minute, then she said slowly, "I know it's none of my business, and I suppose I'm being rude to ask, but are you planning to stay here awhile? You don't have to answer me. It's just that I thought you might be looking for work, and then you said you wanted to ride with me, so I decided you weren't going on through."

"I'll answer your question because I've got one and it's none of my business. I figure on asking the sheriff for the deputy's job."

"No." The word came out of her spontaneously, then her face turned red. "I'm sorry. I shouldn't have said that. The job is open, but I'm wondering if you know what happens to deputies in Converse County."

"Yep, I know. They get shot." He picked up his coffee cup, took a drink, then set it down. "I don't savvy. Fact is, there are a lot of things about this town I don't savvy. Like why you're here and likely not married."

"No, I'm not married," she said. "Like I told you before, I can't get enough money together to get out of town. I'm not married because I'm a Burke, and according to my father and his two brothers who run this county, no man around here is good enough to marry me, so no one has ever asked me." She shrugged and laughed shortly. "I'll have to admit that the picking is pretty slim here anyway."

He didn't say anything more until he finished his steak. He was shocked to hear she was a Burke and more shocked to find a Burke running a hole-in-the-wall eating place like this one. As he pushed back his plate, he said, "I guess you must be related to the sheriff."

"His sister. That's one reason I know you shouldn't take the deputy's job. You'll get killed when it's his job to take chances. You'd better keep riding."

She brought him a slab of custard pie and filled his coffee cup. He said, "I'm sorry I can't take your advice. There's something I've got to do, and I figger it'll be easier to do it if I have the deputy's star. I'll take a chance on getting shot."

"What would bring you to an out-of-the-way, run-down town like Broken Bow?" she asked.

"Now I'll have to say I'm sorry because that ain't none of your business," he said.

"I'm the one who should say I'm sorry. I knew it wasn't any of my business. I shouldn't have asked."

He rose and tossed a coin on the counter. "Now about that ride tomorrow. I hear the sheriff ain't in no real hurry about getting back on Tuesdays."

"Ten o'clock," she said. "I'll meet you at the livery stable."

"Good," he said. "I'll be there." He walked to the door, then paused and looked back. "I guess I'd better tell you my name. It's Mark Morgan."

Her quick smile returned to her lips. "I'm pleased to meet you, Mr. Morgan."

He lifted a hand in a farewell gesture, opened the door, and stepped out into the twilight. He wondered if it would have changed her expression if he had told her his name was Cardigan.

CHAPTER V

Sheriff Allan Burke left Broken Bow on Monday in the middle of the afternoon, taking the Laramie road out of town for about five miles, then swinging northeast. He reached the mountains, climbed West Ridge by a series of switchbacks, and dropped down the east side. He arrived in Bullhide just before dusk.

Burke had made this trip every Monday afternoon for nearly a year. He would, he told himself, have gone completely loco if he had not discovered the pleasure and comfort that Lucy Kline could give him. Now he lived through each week with a steadily increasing anticipation, found that Lucy never disappointed him, and then returned home Tuesday morning, dull of spirit and certain he could not struggle through the following week.

He reined up on the east bank of the creek and sat his saddle for a few minutes as he stared at what remained of Bullhide, feeling sure that Lucy was in her room and watching him. About a generation ago Bullhide had been a small but thriving mining camp. Claims had been strung along a mile of the North Fork which flowed through the narrow valley and then tumbled wildly down the mountain into East Park.

Burke was not old enough to have seen Bullhide in its prime, but he'd heard stories of the gold that had been taken from the creek, the fabulous poker games in the Bullhide Inn, the gunfights, the parlor houses in the upper end of the valley. It had been an exciting camp, and he wished he had been old enough to have come here. Now it was all gone except for the inn, a sprawling two-story stone building that belonged to Lucy's father, Pat Kline.

Burke forded the creek and rode around the inn to the shed in the back. He dismounted and stripped gear from his big bay gelding, fed him, and moved slowly toward the inn, his gaze sweeping the boulder-strewn slope above him for any sign of movement.

He had never run into any of the Hall gang here, and he didn't think he would. Pat Kline had told him he wouldn't. As long as he'd been in office, he'd had a tacit understanding with the Halls that if he let them alone, they would leave him alone, but all the time he'd been quite aware that it was a truce which could not last indefinitely.

Allan Burke was a lawman; the Halls were outlaws, and sooner or later there would have to be a settlement. He was not sure how well they knew his habits, but he suspected that there was very little that went on in Bullhide they didn't know. More than once he had sensed he was being spied on, but he was never sure, and Pat always insisted it was just his imagination.

He went into the inn, nodding at Pat who stood behind the rough pine bar. Pat nodded back. Neither said a word. There was no need to talk. They liked each other, they understood each other, and they needed each other.

Pat was an old man with white hair and a white beard and gnarled hands so crippled with rheumatism that he had trouble holding a bottle as he poured. He had operated the inn during the boom days with the help of his Sioux wife; he had made a fortune and lost it, and now Burke's weekly visits gave him about all the income he received.

Burke laid a ten-dollar gold piece on the bar. Pat picked it up, hefted it, stared at it a moment with love, then slipped it into his pocket, grinning a little as he nodded toward the stairs. Burke climbed the stairs, followed the hall to the front of the building, and opened the door to Lucy's room. He closed the door and leaned against it, staring at her hungrily.

She stood at the window exactly where he had been certain she would be when he had reined his horse up a few minutes before, except that now she had turned so she faced him. She was a tall, slender girl with a body that pleased him in every way. Her hair was black, her skin a light bronze that was a reasonable blend of her mother's copper and her father's white skins.

As usual when he came, she was wearing nothing but a silk Chinese robe embroidered with snarling red dragons. It was slightly open down the front. He had given it to her for Christmas, the only real present he had ever given her. He loved her, and he wished he could marry her.

He was ashamed of the promises he had made to her because he knew he would never be able to take her to Broken Bow and tell his father and uncles that they were married. He would be disinherited immediately.

He hated his father and his uncles, he hated Broken Bow and Converse County, but he could handle his feelings because a fortune was at stake. He didn't think he could ever love Lucy or any other woman enough to give that fortune up.

For a long moment they stood at opposite ends of the room, staring at each other. Then he said softly, "Come here, Lucy." She laughed then as if that was what she had been waiting for, pleased that he still found her attractive, and, holding out her arms, ran to him.

He hugged her, murmuring, "It's been a long week, Lucy, a damned long week."

He kissed her, and, as always, he was able for that moment to forget his dull life in Broken Bow, the tawdry town, his father's domineering nature, his sickly, incompetent uncles. He picked her up and carried her to the bed, and for him there was only this moment, the moment he had lived for all week.

When he woke, it was full dark. The door was open, and the smell of frying meat came to him. Lucy would soon call that supper was ready. He knew he should get up, but he lay there, drowsy, contented, thinking he would like to live the rest of his life this way, satisfied to spend his years in this ghost town with no pressures, no family problems, no knowledge of how the Burke money had been made. If he waited for nature to take its course, he would be a middle-aged man before he possessed the family fortune. Lucy, he knew, would never wait that long.

Aside from Lucy the only person in the world Allan Burke loved was his sister Sharon. He admired her because she had the spunk to defy her father and live her own life. She'd had very little money when she'd had her last blowup with Jess Burke, but that hadn't stopped her. She'd packed a few things, saddled her buckskin, and rode to town.

Sharon had come directly to him in his office and told him what had happened. He'd said she was crazy, that she'd better go back and make up with her father or he'd change his will and cut her off without a cent, but she'd sworn she didn't care. All she wanted was to borrow enough from Al to start a restaurant. Cooking was one of several things she did well.

He had never been able to turn her down on anything she asked of him. He took the money out of his savings account in the bank, giving his uncle Rodney a lie about how he had a chance to buy some valuable town lots in Laramie and he didn't want to miss the opportunity.

Later his father had asked him point-blank if he had loaned Sharon the money to start her business, and he had lied to Jess, too, saying that Sharon had saved enough and had not needed any additional capital. Heaven help him, he thought, if Jess Burke ever found out the truth.

The strangest part of this business was that Jess, who could not bear any sort of opposition or disobedience, ended up admiring Sharon. He even ate his dinner in her restaurant when he was in town at noon, passing the time of day with her as coolly as if they were mere acquaintances.

Jess had never said so, but Allan had a feeling his father despised him in spite of the fact that he had never bucked Jess on anything in his life. Oh, he'd had a few moments of rebellion when he'd thought about giving up his star and leaving the county, but he'd always recovered before he'd had time to carry out any rebellious notions that had come to him.

He rose, lit a lamp, and dressed, wondering how much longer he could hold Lucy and still put off marrying her; how much longer he could avoid telling his father why he left Broken Bow every Monday afternoon. Sooner or later time would run out on both.

He could not bear the thought of losing Lucy; he could not look his father in the eyes and tell him he was going to marry Lucy. Sometimes, he told himself sourly as he went down the stairs, it would be simpler to shoot himself in the head and leave his troubles behind him.

Lucy was standing at the range frying steak when he entered the kitchen. He walked up behind her, put his arms around her, and cupped both breasts in his hands as he kissed her on the back of her neck. She shivered and turned her head enough for him to see her smile.

"I thought you'd be hungry enough to get up pretty soon," she said, "but I was beginning to think I'd have to call you."

"I smelled supper," he said.

"It's as good as a dinner bell." She paused, then she said vehemently, "Al, I've never been out of Converse County, and I've only been to Broken Bow once. If I don't look out, I'll be an old maid and I'll have lived in Bullhide all my life."

"You've got a ways to go," he said.

"Well, I don't feel like it," she snapped. "When are you going to marry me?"

He released her and walked to the table and sat down. He rolled a smoke, realizing she was very angry, that just maybe she had reached the end of her patience. He said slowly, "Damn it, Lucy, I want to marry you so bad I can taste it. I will marry you as soon as I talk it over with pa and my uncles. It's just that lately pa ain't been in no mood to talk to."

"He hasn't been from the first day you came here to see me," she said in a tight, carefully controlled voice. "I'm beginning to think he never will be. You're twenty-nine years old, Allan Burke. You're old enough to start acting like a man."

It was true and it hurt. He stared at the cigarette in his fingers, not saying anything for a time. He thought again of Sharon and her telling their father what he could do with his money as far as she was concerned. It irritated him that he still did not know whether Jess Burke had changed his will leaving everything to him or not, but it wouldn't have surprised him if his father had not changed the will and Sharon still got half.

"I've told you and I'll tell you again," he said finally, "that the Burke fortune adds up to more than one hundred thousand dollars. Someday I'll get all of it. When I do, I'll keep every promise I ever made to you."

She said nothing more for a time but remained at the stove stirring the gravy, her back straight and tense the way it always was when she was furious. He had not seen her that way very often, but he had known for some time that she was capable of almost anything when she was in a rage.

She did not blow up and scream at him as she had in the past when she was this angry. She said in that same controlled voice, "Call pa."

He stepped into the front of the house and motioned to Pat as he said, "Come and get it," and returned to the kitchen.

A moment later the old man came in and sat down. They ate in silence. Pat seldom said anything, and tonight the chilly atmosphere froze the conversation that would normally have flowed between Burke and Lucy. When they finished the steak and potatoes, Lucy brought a chocolate cake out of the pantry and cut an unusually liberal slice for Al.

"I'm sorry," she said as she passed his piece of cake to him. "It seems that I've waited so long. Sometimes I think I can't spend another day in this hellhole."

"I'll talk to pa this week," he promised and knew he wouldn't.

She patted his arm and smiled contritely. "Hurry up and eat," she said.

"Why the hell should he?" Pat asked. "You've got all night, ain't you?"

"I'm tired of waiting for anything," she flared. "I've been waiting for something all my life. I'm not going to do it much longer."

The old man chuckled. "Larry Hall will take you somewhere if you'll let him. I dunno where it'll be, but it won't be anywhere around Bullhide."

"What's this about Larry Hall?" Burke demanded.

"I'll tell you later," Lucy said. "Go on. Eat your cake."

Pat finished and rose. "Come into the bar and I'll give you a drink."

In the year that Burke had been coming here, Pat Kline had seldom if ever offered him a free drink. He rose, suddenly curious, and paused when Lucy said, "One drink, Al. Just one."

When he reached the bar, Pat had already poured

42

his drink and had put the bottle away. He said, "I wanted to tell you that I seen the Dorn kids ride by this afternoon toward town."

"What does that mean?"

"I dunno," Pat said. "But I tell you those punk kids just scare the hell out of me, and I've handled some purty tough hombres in my day. The last time they was in here, I ran 'em out with a shotgun. They ain't just ornery. They're goddamn mean, the kind of meanness that makes 'em skin a dog while he's alive just to hear him howl. I sure didn't like the way they looked at Lucy the last time they was in here. They ain't human, Al. They're animals."

Burke turned his glass with his fingertips, thinking that he had heard stories like that about the Dorns, but he had never had reason to tangle with them, so he'd thought the stories were exaggerated. They were young: seventeen, eighteen, and nineteen. They had made their own living since their father had been killed in a drunken brawl five years ago, a poor living hunting and trapping that was just one jump ahead of starvation.

"I've seen 'em in town lots of times," Burke said slowly, "but I never knew 'em to do anything very ornery."

"Then maybe you never looked real close," Pat said testily. "They worship the Halls and want to throw in with 'em, but the old man don't want no truck with 'em. Now I'll tell you something else. I seen 'em ride by here every one of the days when you had a deputy killed."

Burke stared at the old man, then nodded. "You know, I've thought of that, but I figured they were just wild kids who wouldn't do anything like that."

"They would," Pat said, "and I figure they did."

"How come they knock over my deputies and not me?" Burke asked.

"Old man Hall put out the word you're not to be touched," Pat said. "He figures it's better to keep you alive wearing the star than to have you dead and somebody else sheriff. I guess he likes the way you run the county."

"Well, I don't do much running," Burke said, "and I guess that's the way he likes it. What's this about Larry Hall taking Lucy out of Bullhide?"

"Didn't mean nothing," Pat said, "with Lucy crazy about you the way she is, but awhile back Larry asked her to marry him. Seems like they're planning one more big caper in Wyoming, and then they're lighting out for Mexico. He wants her to go with him, but I've been bucking it. I don't cotton to the notion of her running all over the country with a gang of outlaws."

Pat paused, his faded eyes narrowed as he studied Burke, then he said, "I'll tell you something, Al. You're gonna have to do it or get off the pot. She ain't gonna wait much longer."

Burke wheeled away from the bar, leaving his drink untouched. As he crossed the kitchen and climbed the stairs, he had trouble breathing. He felt as if a horse had kicked him in the belly.

CHAPTER VI

The only saloon in town was O'Hara's Bar two doors from the hotel. Mark stopped there for a drink before he went to bed, wondering if it, too, was owned by one of the Burkes. A little competition would bring some improvements in Broken Bow, but obviously the Burkes did not look with favor upon any threat of competition.

He found O'Hara's Bar just about what he had expected. He paused for a moment inside the batwings, noting the scarred pine bar on the left side of the room, the shelves back of the bar which held a bigger array of bottles than he expected, and four green-topped tables on the right side of the room, each with four chairs. There was no chandelier hanging from the ceiling. The only light was from a few bracket kerosene lamps on the walls.

Two cowboys were playing cards at the front table. Three men were lounging at the back table. The other two tables were unoccupied. These five were the only ones in the saloon except for Mark and the bartender, a big-bellied old man of about the same age as the courthouse janitor, the stableman, and the hotel clerk. A dreary atmosphere pervaded the saloon, the same dreary atmosphere, Mark thought, that hung over the entire town of Broken Bow.

He walked to the bar, nodding at the bartender who nodded back. Mark said, "Whiskey," and the bartender nodded again. He took a bottle from a shelf, poured the drink, and returned the bottle to the shelf.

"The best in the house," the bartender said. "You look like a man who wouldn't settle for less."

Mark paid for the drink, not certain what kind of remark was called for, so he said nothing. The bartender stared at him speculatively for a time, then he asked, "Just riding through?"

"Not exactly," Mark answered, "if it's any of your business, which it ain't."

"Oh, it's my business, all right," the bartender said. "I like the cut of your jib, and I just got to thinking you might be a man the sheriff had sent for to serve as deputy. We need one bad. Maybe you heard that the last three deputies had been gunned down."

"I heard."

"Well, did Al Burke send for you?"

"No."

The bartender sighed, plainly disappointed. "Hell, we sure need a good man, one who can stay alive. Al, he's all right, but he ain't one to slap the lid on and keep it there. Besides, he's out of town a lot, and when he's gone, we don't have nobody to look after things."

"The town seems quiet enough," Mark said.

"Most of the time it is," the bartender agreed, "but about the time we're ready to dig the grave, all hell breaks loose." He leaned forward and said in a low tone, "Take them bratty kids at the back table. They're

the Dorns. Might as well have three wild animals in
here when they get going. Better keep an eye on 'em,
friend. They've been looking you over ever since you
came in. They figger that any stranger who walks in
here alone is their meat."

Mark turned, wondering if the barman was trying
to stir up some excitement to enliven a dull evening.
The cowboys at the front table were still playing cards
and paying no attention to anyone else in the room,
but the three at the back table had their heads together, snickering and talking in low tones, their eyes
on Mark.

The light was too thin for Mark to make them out
clearly, but he could see they were young, that they
were wearing buckskin clothes that looked homemade,
and that they had grown the wispy beards and mus-
taches of youths who were trying to look like men a
year or two before they were.

Suddenly one of the boys slammed his hand down
against the table and shouted, "By God, I can handle
him. He don't look like much to me."

He rose, took a hitch on his belt, and swaggered
across the room toward Mark, the other two watching
and grinning as if they were anticipating the sport
ahead of time. It was an old game to Mark, a game he
had seen played more than once in Springfield by local
bullies, baiting a stranger who happened to wander
into a saloon by himself. There was only one way to
respond. The result was often tragedy for the man
who didn't know how or when to pick up his end.

"Let him alone, kid," the bartender said as if he
didn't expect to be obeyed. "He's just passing through."

"Shut up, you old goat," young Dorn said and tipped

his head forward in Mark's direction. "That right? What he said about your passing through?"

Mark didn't answer for a moment. He stood relaxed as he surveyed the boy, his hands at his sides, his back to the bar. The kid wore a gun on his right side, a knife on his left. He had a thin, wolfish face with cruel lips that were slightly parted showing rows of chipped, dirty teeth.

Now that he was close, Mark choked on the smell of him, not just the stink of an unwashed body, but the smell of a man who lives in filth. Mark had known men in Springfield who lived that way and carried the same stomach-churning smell. The buffalo hunters were gone by the time Mark grew up, but he had been told by older settlers that they had the same smell.

"I asked you a question," the boy snarled, his left hand dropping to the handle of his knife. "Now goddamn it, you'd better answer me."

The kid stood no more than three feet from him. He was leaning forward, a sudden frenzy taking hold of him. Mark moved fast, grabbing young Dorn's left wrist and yanking him around in one swift, savage movement, his left arm slipping under the boy's chin and closing in on his windpipe as his right hand twisted the kid's arm behind his back, bringing it up until it was just short of being broken.

The brothers at the table were motionless for a moment, surprised into immobility by what Mark had done, then they jumped to their feet, hands moving toward the butts of their guns. The cowboys at the front table rose, dropped their cards, and strode out of the saloon. The Dorn boy who had started the row squirmed and kicked in a futile effort to free himself, but he was smaller than Mark and not as strong, and he didn't accomplish anything except to hurt his arm more than it had been.

"You boys try making a play with your guns," Mark said, "and you'll wind up shooting your brother, which same won't make no never mind if I choke him to death first, which I'm of a mind to do."

They froze, their guns barely clear of leather. The boy Mark held had quit his struggling. He tried to say something about not having done anything to Mark, but Mark increased the pressure on his throat until his face started to turn purple and all he could do was to mumble and gasp.

"Drop your guns back into leather," Mark snapped, "and then head for the door. I'm clean out of patience."

They hesitated, then eased their guns back into their holsters and stalked toward the batwings. Mark followed, pushing his captive ahead of him until they were outside on the boardwalk. Then Mark released his grip on the boy's throat and wrist and, bringing his knee up into young Dorn's butt, slammed him forward. He staggered for several steps, then lost his balance and fell forward on his face.

Mark drew his gun. "Git on your horses and vamoose," he said. "I aim to be around Broken Bow for a while. The next time you try to have some sport with me will be the last time you try it on anybody."

All three were in their saddles then. The one who had been Mark's captive said in a croaking voice, "I'll kill you, mister. I'm gonna kill you."

They dug in their spurs and left town on the run. Mark watched them until they disappeared in the darkness, then he returned to the saloon. The bartender was wiping his face with his bandanna. He held out a hand and Mark shook it, grinning a little.

"You done good," the bartender said. "Damned good."

"What did you expect me to do?" Mark asked. "Stand there and let the three of 'em work me over?"

"Most men would have," the barman answered. "I mean, most men don't know what's coming and figure they can handle whichever Dorn makes the play. How'd you know what they'd do?"

"I've seen toughs play the game before," Mark said. "You sail into the one who starts the fracas, figuring it'll be a fair fight, then the others move in using knives or gun barrels or anything they can get their hands on and beat hell out of you. I've seen men damned near killed by three or four who gang up on him for no reason."

"That's the way the Dorns work," the bartender said, "and the only reason they do it is just for the fun of it. You're the first man I ever seen handle 'em. Bud, he's the one you tangled with, didn't figure on you making a move when you did. He's the youngest and the meanest. I guess he grew up fighting the other two."

"What kind of jaspers are they?" Mark asked. "Don't they have any parents?"

The bartender shook his head. "Their pa was killed right here in this room about five years ago. Their ma was already dead. They live in the mountains on the other side of Bullhide, and they've made it on their own ever since the old man got beefed. Oh, I guess the Halls and some of the others up there have helped 'em some, but they raised themselves like a litter of wolves. They run like a pack of wolves, too. You'd better watch 'em if you stay around here. They don't forget."

"I'll watch 'em," Mark said. "Good night."

He left the saloon and walked to the hotel, thinking sourly that he'd got himself into trouble with three young toughs who had nothing to do with his purpose for coming to Converse County. Well, one thing was sure. He'd see to it that they didn't interfere with his reason for coming.

CHAPTER VII

The steady beat of hoofs was coming closer and closer. Someone was pounding on the door. A man was calling, "Wake up and dress, Kate. They're coming. I'll saddle your horse." A woman in a white nightgown was dressing and taking him out of bed and was dressing him. Then she was outside holding him in her arms and a man was saying, "Hand the boy up to me." They were riding, but the beat of hoofs behind them was unrelenting and steadily coming closer and closer.

Mark sat up in bed and put his feet on the floor. He was wet with sweat; he was trembling and weak, and it took him a moment to find the strength to get up and cross the room to the bureau. He poured water from the pitcher into the basin; he washed and dried his face, then found his shirt and took tobacco and paper from the pocket and rolled a cigarette. He moved the chair to the window and watched the day come, the cool dawn air washing over him.

He hadn't solved his problem by coming to East Park, he thought sourly. He had hoped that once he was actually here, the nightmares would stop plaguing him, but this last one had been the most complete and terrifying he'd ever had.

Aunt Kate had told him what had happened; the nightmares were clearly the result of what had happened that terrifying night, a frightening experience that he had forgotten but still had stored in some secret pocket of his mind.

He'd had doubts about what Aunt Kate had told him for some reason which he could not identify. Now that he was here in East Park, he would confirm what she had told him or he would disprove it. He would start this morning with Sharon.

When full light had come, he dressed and, leaving the hotel, walked the length of Main Street. Knowing that Sharon's restaurant wouldn't be open at this hour, he cruised the side streets, noting that most of the houses were log cabins or small, white cottages.

He found two houses that were different, palaces when compared to the others. They were large, with mansard roofs and iron fences around the yards and carriage houses in the back. Both were painted white with bright red trim. They would, he thought, belong to Bob Burke, the storekeeper, and Rodney Burke, the banker.

He was reminded of company towns he had read about in which the owners resided in fine houses and the workers lived in shacks. This situation did not fit the cattle country he had known where people were as equal as it was possible to be in any human society, and he wondered what sort of men the Burkes were who had established it here.

By the time he reached Main Street, Sharon's Beanery was open, but Sharon wasn't there. A middle-aged woman, white haired and pleasant faced, was behind the counter. She took his order of ham and eggs and coffee and brought his breakfast to him in a surprisingly short time.

The woman did not attempt to carry on a conversation, and Mark was glad because he didn't feel like talking. He finished his meal and paid, and as he left, he passed the stableman and the hotel clerk who were coming in for breakfast.

He returned to his room, shaved, and put on a clean shirt, deciding that Broken Bow was more like an old Southern plantation than a company town. Maybe the people who lived here weren't slaves, but they weren't far from it.

Obviously the Burkes took care of their people by giving them work and paying them enough to live on. It was to the Burkes' credit that no one was starving. Still he was offended because it seemed to him that the Burkes controlled the town and the county and the lives of the people who worked for them. Sharon was probably the only one in town who had successfully defied the Burke brothers, and the only reason she survived was the fact that she was Jess Burke's daughter.

He was in the livery stable a few minutes before ten o'clock and had saddled his sorrel by the time Sharon came in. She said, "Good morning," and nodded at him as Mark said, "Good morning."

She was, he thought, even more attractive this morning than she had been the night before in the restaurant. She wore a dark green riding skirt, a leather jacket, and a broad-brimmed hat held in place by a chin strap. She seemed happy, he thought, even a little excited, and he told himself hopefully that it was because she was riding with him. He almost laughed aloud at his temerity.

Sharon gave his sorrel a quick appraisal and nodded. "He's a good-looking horse," she said, "but I wouldn't trade you." She nodded at the buckskin the stableman was cinching up. "I call him Bugeye for no reason. My father gave him to me when I was twelve. I couldn't live without him. He's the only way I have of getting away from town for an hour or so every day."

A moment later the stableman led the buckskin along the runway to Sharon. When he reached her, he said something in a low tone that Mark couldn't catch. Sharon shook her head at the stableman and laughed as she said, "I never saw a man I couldn't handle."

"Even Larry Hall?"

"Even Larry Hall," she said. "You ready to ride, Mr. Morgan?"

"He's a stranger," the stableman said doggedly. "Damn it, Sharon, your pa will have a fit when he hears about it."

"Maybe he won't hear," Sharon said. "Anyhow, he has a fit every day for one reason or another." She mounted and rode through the archway into the street, jerking her head for Mark to follow.

Mark said to the stableman, "She's safe with me, mister. You tell her dad that if you see him before we get back."

He was in a sour mood when he caught up with Sharon who had turned north on Main Street. He said, "I guess I look like an evil man to that old goat."

"It's a typical Burke attitude," she said grimly, "that no one is good enough for a Burke. It's the reason my brother never married. It's all right for him to sleep with a woman but not to marry her. It's also the reason I'm going to get out of here. I don't intend to be an old maid all my life."

Her grim mood changed as suddenly as it had come. She flashed Mark a smile. "I'll race you to the bridge," she said and dug in her spurs before he had a chance to accept or refuse her challenge.

She beat him by a full length, largely because she had got the jump on him. She pulled up after they had thundered across the bridge, calling, "I told you I wouldn't swap my horse for yours."

"Well, now," he said, "I don't think you proved anything. It would have been different if it had been a longer race. Besides, you didn't give me . . ."

He stopped, feeling her mocking gaze on him. "You're a bad loser," she said, "and now you're alibiing."

"Oh, I'm a bad loser, all right," he agreed. "I like to win. I'll be in a very bad mood if I don't get the deputy's job."

"Oh, you'll get it, all right," she said. "Al will be glad to get a new deputy. Then you can take the risks and do the dying for him."

"I get the notion you're not very fond of your brother," Mark said.

She shook her head. "No, I like him very much. He's always been good to me. When I left home, I didn't have enough money, and I knew there was no use going to the bank. Uncle Rodney wouldn't have loaned me a nickel as soon as he found out I was bucking pa, and he would have found out before he made the loan, so I went to Al and he got it for me."

She hesitated, staring straight ahead, then she said

slowly, "I'd better tell you about Al. It might save you some time and maybe keep you from taking risks you shouldn't take. Al is a very persuasive man. He's pleasant to be around and to talk to, but he's mostly mush when it gets down to a situation where he has to be tough. He claims he's a coward, but he's not. It's just that he's short on backbone. For him it's simpler to go along with what pa and his brothers want than it is to fight them. I get a little disgusted with him because of that. Someday somebody has to make some changes in Converse County, and it would be too bad to have to wait until pa and my uncles die of old age. My father is a very healthy man."

Again she hesitated, glancing sideways at him as if trying to make up her mind how much she should tell. He said, "I think there's more. Go ahead. Tell me."

"I hate being a tattletale," she said, "but you're a stranger and you don't understand the politics of the county, or the Burke greed. To my father and uncles this is their little empire and they run it to suit themselves, and they simply smash anyone who stands up to them.

"Al could have got married a couple years ago. There was a very nice schoolteacher Al liked. I guess she liked him, too, the way she acted; but pa said she wasn't the kind of woman to be a Burke wife. She was a little older than Al and rather plain looking, so they fired her after one year, and Al didn't say much. If it had been me, I'd have gone with her when she left the park."

"I see," he said and wondered if taking the deputy's star in Converse County was being smart or stupid. "I'm curious about him being gone every Monday afternoon. Last night I had a run-in with the Dorn boys, and the bartender said the sheriff was gone every Monday and that left no one here in town to handle anything that came up."

"I heard about your trouble with the Dorns," she said. "I understand you set them on their ears. It's time someone did. They're vicious. They usually show up in town on Monday nights when he's gone, so he never sees any of their shenanigans. I think you're exactly the kind of man Converse County needs."

"Why does he leave?" Mark asked. "Where does he go and what does he do?"

"It's the worst-kept secret in the county," she said. "He goes to Bullhide. It's an old mining camp that is deserted except for Pat Kline who runs the inn there. He has a half-breed daughter that Al has been sleeping with. At least that's the gossip. Al has never talked about it to me, and no one mentions it to him. Pa doesn't object to Al seeing the girl, but if Al decided to marry her, pa would raise hell and prop it up with a chunk."

"I see," Mark said.

The more he heard about Al Burke, the less he thought he would either like or respect him. This business of disappearing twenty-four hours on the same afternoons and mornings of every week was incredible and stupid, and it left the town wide open for anyone who wanted to hit the bank or do anything else that was criminal.

Mark didn't tell Sharon what he thought. He knew it would destroy the good beginning he had made with her, and he had more important things to do than upset her and make her angry. She seemed willing to talk, and he had a good deal in mind for her to talk about if he could get her off the subject of her relatives.

"I've heard about a family that lived here in the early days named Cardigan," he said casually. "Ever hear of them?"

"Yes, I've heard of them," she said, again giving him her questioning look. "How did you happen to be interested in them?"

"Oh, they're relatives of mine," he said, "so I was curious about where they lived and what happened to them."

"They lived in Cardigan valley," she said. "It's just west of here. Want to see it?"

"Yes, I would," he said. "Like I just told you, I'm curious about them."

"It's my guess it's more than curiosity," she said tartly, "and it's time you told me a little bit about yourself."

"Sure," he said. "I don't have any dark secrets to hide."

"Go ahead," she said. "Tell me."

"All in good time," he said. "No hurry."

"I'm not a patient woman." She motioned to the left. "We turn here. I'll make a deal with you. I'll tell you anything you want, but I want to know why."

He hesitated, not sure how much he should tell her. Still she was probably the best source of information he could find, so he nodded. "You've got a deal," he said.

CHAPTER VIII

Mark rode beside Sharon to the top of a long ridge. She pulled up, motioning for him to stop as she nodded toward the valley below them. She said, "That's it."

He sat in his saddle for a time, staring at the valley. A small, willow-lined stream meandered back and forth, reaching as far as he could see to the west. Most of the valley floor was covered by grass, rich green in the bright sunlight, with here and there the brown bulk of one of last year's haystacks. Only the bordering hills held the somber gray of sagebrush.

Directly below them was a grove of cottonwoods that had been there long before the Burkes or the Cardigans or any of the others had arrived in East Park with their wagons and cattle. Here in the shade of the big trees was what looked like the remains of a house. Below it were the barn and corrals.

"Let's take a closer look," he said.

"Is it what you expected?" Sharon asked as they started down the slope.

"It's bigger than I thought it would be," he said, "and prettier. It's a beautiful ranch site."

"It's the best in the park," she said. "That's the

reason pa wanted it, although he never moved his headquarters here. I'm not sure why, unless it was the stories about the Cardigans haunting this valley after they were killed. Pa's not a superstitious man, but there's something about this valley that gets to him. He never comes here any more, not even when they're haying." She shrugged, then added, "Anyhow, it's the best meadowland in the park, and he gets a good hay crop from it every year."

"Did he run other people out of the valley?"

She laughed, a harsh sound that held no humor. "He surely did. He ran them out or he shot them like he did the Cardigans or they got scared and left."

"There must be other people here beside the Burkes," he said.

"Sure," she agreed. "They either work for the Burkes or they're the submissive ones who live by Burke law and never think of rebelling. They own ten-cow spreads in the edges and corners of the park, places where the soil is shallow and where the grass is not as good as the land pa controls."

"In other words," Mark said, "he took his pick, and the others live here only because he lets them."

"That's right," she said. "They help pa when he needs help like during roundup or haying or when they make the drive to Laramie in the fall. They take along half a dozen of their steers, so they work for nothing. They buy what they have to have in Uncle Bob's store and they borrow money from Uncle Rodney's bank and they are always in debt. The bank can take their places any time pa decides he wants one of their spreads or gets sore at one of them—which he does once in a while."

They reached the bottom of the hill and splashed

across the creek, a clear, slow-moving stream that carried ample water to irrigate the valley, and reined up under one of the cottonwoods. Mark dismounted and for a time stood looking at what remained of the Cardigan buildings. Nothing was left of the house but the stone walls, and they had crumbled until they looked more like a rectangular pile of rocks than the remains of a ranch house.

Mark judged that the barn had been used recently. The log walls were intact, but the roof sagged, one door hung askew from the top hinge, and the glass had been knocked out of the small, cobweb-covered windows. The corrals were intact and probably were used every fall after the hay was cut and stacked and the cattle brought down from the upper pastures and allowed to graze here. The privy had been knocked over on its side, and several other small buildings had been flattened so that nothing remained but piles of weathered boards and shingles.

Sharon had dismounted and, walking to the nearest corral, sat down with her back to the logs. He felt her eyes on him as he prowled around the ruins of the house, but she said nothing. He stepped inside the walls. Grass had grown up in the rubble so he found nothing except two rusty stoves that had survived the twenty years since it had been occupied. Then he remembered Aunt Kate telling him that the house had been burned.

Mark thought he could make out the plan of the house. For a time he stood in what he judged to be the living room and closed his eyes, trying to bring back into his mind the reality of the nightmare. Aunt Kate would have stood about where he was standing now when Ed Cardigan had shouted to her to get dressed. Suddenly he could hear the pound of hoofs; he felt prickles rush down his spine and chill him as the fear which had accompanied every nightmare flooded his body again, momentarily paralyzing him just as it had a few hours before.

He opened his eyes and moved through what must have been the front door. Once more he stood motionless with his eyes closed, sweat breaking through his skin as it had every time one of the nightmares had wakened him. He didn't move for several minutes. Presently he heard Ed Cardigan's voice clearly, "Hand the boy up to me."

When he opened his eyes again and wiped his face with his bandanna the moment had passed. He was here as a man, a man who could hold the Burkes accountable for the crimes they had committed. This time, he told himself, the nightmares were really over. He had come to their source, the spell was broken, and he was free. He felt as if a great cloud that had thrown its shadow over him for so long was gone. At last he knew what had happened, and he knew what he had to do.

He walked to where Sharon sat beside the corral and dropped to the ground beside her. He took the makings from his pocket and rolled a smoke, his fingers trembling. He did not look at the girl, but he sensed that she was staring at him, measuring him, perhaps judging him, but he said nothing to her unspoken question.

"You look as if you'd been there and couldn't get back," she said. "Seeing this place has done something to you. I think it's time you kept your part of our bargain."

63

"I've got a question or two first," he said. "You don't love your father much, do you?"

"Why should I love a son of a bitch who by an accident of nature became my father?" she demanded passionately. "I choose my friends. I'll choose the man I marry. I did not choose Jess Burke as my father."

"Then you hate him," Mark said. "Why?"

"Hate him?" she said in a questioning tone. "I don't know that I can say that. Just because I don't love him doesn't mean I hate him." She paused, frowning. "It's a funny thing, now that you put it that way. I've never thought about hating him. I knew I didn't love him, and he's always demanded love just as he always demanded it from the women he kept in our home. To him love was obedience."

She paused, staring at the ruins of the Cardigan house, and, Mark thought, not seeing it. Finally she said, "I guess I do hate him, not because of what he's done to me as much as what he's done to other people."

She motioned to the pile of rock. "The Cardigans. The Halls. The Dorns. Even my uncles. He's the youngest of the family, so it's opposite to what it's supposed to be, but he gives the orders. He's beaten them into line time after time. They're afraid of him, really physically afraid."

"Tell me what brought this on," he said, motioning to the ruins of the house.

"It happened just about the time I was born," she said, "so all I know is what I've heard, and there are a lot of different stories. The one that seems most likely is that the Cardigans were good cowmen. They were tough, and when the Burkes began putting different kinds of pressure on people to get their land, the

Cardigans resisted. Even old man Hall who is now considered a very bad man caved in and moved out of the park.

"At that time pa had a woman living with him named Marta. She was very beautiful, I hear, and I have a feeling that she was the only woman pa ever loved. In his way, I mean. He was always hard on women. He gave them a good house, good food, and fine dresses, but he was hard on them.

"Some of the women resisted him, some submitted. Al's mother died when he was five. Later my mother got on a train and left without saying anything to anyone. I don't have the slightest idea where she is now. One thing I will say for pa. He raised Al and me. My mother didn't give a damn about what happened to me, so it's a good thing pa had enough responsibility to take care of me until I could look out for myself.

"This Marta I mentioned was different. She moved in with the Cardigans and married the older one, Flint. From that time on pa hated the Cardigans. He didn't hate the other people he drove out of the park, but he hated the Cardigans. He tried everything he could to get at them, but nothing worked. Then Marta had a baby and died. Pa blamed Flint for that, but for some reason he waited three years before he decided to end it."

Sharon picked up a stick and began making marks in the dirt. A minute or more passed before she said, "This part of the story gets pretty bad. I don't really know what happened. There are so many different versions, but one thing was sure. Pa decided to kill Flint Cardigan. He sent for a couple of gunmen who jumped Flint. Flint killed both of them.

"I guess after that pa allowed he'd better do the job himself. He cornered Flint in O'Hara's Bar with some of his crew and shot Flint to pieces. Ed had gone out through the back. He looked in and saw what had happened and ran. He must have come here. You see, they had sent for a woman to keep house. Some say she was Marta's sister. I think pa would have killed her and the boy, but by the time they got here, the woman and the boy were gone."

Sharon looked at Mark and spread her hands as if telling him she didn't know what happened after that. "All I know is that the woman and boy were seen getting on the train. I don't think anybody around here knows what happened to them, but Ed Cardigan's body was found about a couple of miles out of town."

Sharon took a long breath. "Now it's your turn. What's your interest in this?"

Mark rolled a cigarette and fired it. He said, "What you've told me is what I came here to find out. Now I can ride back to where I came from."

"But you won't," she said. "You want the deputy's job. Why? I don't believe it's just the hundred dollars a month."

He needed time to think. He was not a vengeful man, but here was a wrong that cried out for justice. If he didn't see that it was done, no one ever would. Besides, this valley was rightfully his. The question, he decided, was whether he could trust Sharon with the truth. If she went to her father with it, he would be murdered just as Flint and Ed Cardigan had been murdered.

"Well?" Sharon said impatiently.

"If I tell you why I'm here and if I stay which I aim

to do for a while," he said, "you would have the power of life and death over me."

She was shocked. "I don't want that, but if it has anything to do with pa which I figure it has, you can depend on one thing. I'll never tell him."

"All right," he said. "The woman you mentioned, Marta, was my mother."

CHAPTER IX

When Al Burke was ready to leave the Bullhide Inn Tuesday morning, Lucy hugged and kissed him, saying, "Don't forget. You're talking to your father this week. I won't wait any longer." Then she put her mouth close to his ear and whispered, "I'm carrying your baby, Al."

She drew back and looked at him, a small smile on her lips. For a moment he thought he had misunderstood her, but he knew at once he hadn't. She was not ashamed; she seemed happy about it. He was sick then, a crazy kind of sickness that turned his belly to jelly. He sat down on one of the kitchen chairs and stared at her as if seeing her for the first time in his life. A baby was the last thing he wanted, a baby who would probably be as dark skinned as Lucy.

"Why are you so shocked?" she asked. "You've given me plenty of opportunity to start a baby. If you didn't want one, you shouldn't have been coming here to see me." She stopped, then asked slyly, "You have been enjoying your visits, haven't you?"

"Yes," he said hoarsely. "I've been enjoying them,

all right, and so have you, but I didn't want a baby. Not yet."

"No, not as long as you could put off marrying me," she said. "But you can't do that any longer. We've got to get married. I'm giving you this week. No more. If you aren't ready to marry me by next Monday, I'll see your father myself, and I'll tell him about us. I want to get married before I begin to show. That's not being unreasonable, is it?"

"No, it isn't," he agreed. "I'll see you next Monday."

He rose and strode through the bar, not looking back at her. Pat Kline caught up with him and walked around the building to the shed where Burke had left his horse. Kline said, "There's something else I ought to tell you. I reckon you ain't one to scare easy, but I'd better tell you."

"If it's about Lucy, you can save your wind. She just told me."

Kline shook his head. "I didn't mean that. We talked enough about it last night. I take you for an honorable man who would do right by Lucy. If you didn't there's always Larry Hall. He'd take her any way any time, but I figured you love her enough not to let that happen. I've got to provide for her future someway 'cause I don't have many years left."

Burke glanced at the old man, then lifted his saddle to his horse's back. "I'll take care of her," he said and meant it.

"I'm talking now about the Halls," Kline said. "The last time they was here, they got to drinking purty hard, enough to loosen the old man's tongue. I reckon you know how much he hates all the Burkes, Jess in particular. He sure never made any secret of it. He's been living up there in that canyon all these years just letting his hate grow until it's poisoned him. Well, now the Halls are fixing to leave the country, but the old man says they ain't going until they finish the Burkes."

"They'll have a hard time doing that," Burke said as he stepped into the saddle.

"I ain't as sure as you are," Kline said, "and I ain't interested either way except for Lucy's sake I'd like to keep you alive long enough to marry her. Now you count 'em up. There's the four Halls. They'll have the Dorn kids. That's seven. I figger they'll pick up two, three more, young bucks who are looking for some excitement. That makes maybe ten. They aim to burn the town. Now just how are you going to stop 'em with that bunch of old men you've got living in Broken Bow?"

Burke drew in a long breath, wondering why after all this time his world was falling down around him. "Why has the old man waited twenty years?" he asked.

Kline shrugged. "Who knows? Maybe his hate hadn't got big enough until now. Or maybe it's 'cause they're leaving the country and the old man knows if they don't do it now, they'll never do it."

"When are they coming?"

"How the hell do I know?" Kline snapped. "I ain't in on their schemes. I just overheard some of their talk. Seems like the caper in Wyoming is a train hold-up, and they're waiting for word about when a gold shipment is coming through. My guess is it'll be in a week or two."

"I'll watch out for 'em," Burke said and rode past the inn and on across the creek.

70

It wasn't until he topped West Ridge and was on his way down that his head cleared and he began to think clearly, first about Lucy, then about the Halls. He often hated himself when he stopped to think about how he had bowed to his father and licked his boots ever since he was big enough to know that was what Jess Burke wanted. It was something that Sharon had never done, and he told himself glumly that she was happier because she'd defied her father.

Still he had his personal hard core of morals that he had never violated. He never knew just why he was this way, but he had told himself all along that there were some things he could not do even for Jess Burke. By the same token there were some things he would do regardless of the cost.

Honor, he told himself grimly, was not something that had solid lines and could be defined, but one thing was sure. His definition of honor would not permit a man to father a child and then refuse to accept the responsibility for that child. In this regard his father had been an honorable man when he had raised both him and Sharon, something that other men, who were not murderers and thieves as his father was, might have refused to do.

He knew that many men, if they were in his boots, would have told Lucy to go to hell and gone away and forgotten her, particularly since she was a half-breed, but he could not do that. He had come to the end of the road. If it meant giving up the Burke fortune, then that's the way it would have to be, no matter how painful it was. He would tell his father about Lucy. He would say he was going to marry her. He had a little money in the bank, and maybe Sharon could pay back what he had loaned her. He still had more than a year to go on his job as sheriff, and he would have his salary as sheriff for that long. Jess Burke could not take it from him.

For a moment he let his thoughts linger on Lucy and how it would be when they were married. Sharon, he knew, would accept her, but probably no one else in Broken Bow would. Well, it didn't make any difference. Lucy was used to being alone. She'd make a good wife. That was all he could ask.

He turned his thoughts then to the Hall gang. Kline had been dead right in saying he couldn't defend the town with the old men who lived there. The only fighting men in the county who could do the job were the Bar B hands, but they were scattered all over East Park.

Jess never liked to let anything interfere with ranch work, but he certainly couldn't refuse to bring them in to save Broken Bow. The trouble was Burke had no way of knowing when the Halls would strike, and for the crew to lie around town for days doing nothing was unthinkable.

Still there was no other way. He had to ask Jess for the men. The only alternative to waiting in town for the raid was to take the Bar B men as a posse and go after the Halls. They couldn't burn Broken Bow if they were in jail. He'd have to think of some charge he could hold them on.

When he was a mile from town, he turned off to the Bar B, his stomach feeling queasy. He didn't like to ask his father for anything. Now to ask him for men and then tell him about Lucy was too much, but he had to face it.

He reined up in front of the Bar B ranch house just before noon, dismounted, and tied. It was a sprawling building; the middle portion was two-story and made of stone, the wings on each end were constructed of logs. He had been a boy when the wings were built. He remembered the construction well, hanging around the carpenters and watching everything they did.

Now, for nearly twenty years, there had been no change. The big barn with the weather vane on the roof, a white horse that could be seen half a mile away, the corrals, the outbuildings: all were marks of a rich and prosperous working ranch. Too, in appearance it was a man's ranch. None of the women who had lived here had left her mark on the place.

His gaze ranged over the familiar scene; he saw that everything was in order as it always was. He had not been here for months, but he could have drawn this scene from memory and not missed a thing.

He walked up the path to the front door and, opening the screen, stepped into the big living room. He smelled dinner and crossed the room to the kitchen. Bertha, Jess's housekeeper and bed partner, was frying steak at the stove. She had lived here for more than five years, a middle-aged woman who was not particularly attractive but was efficient. Apparently she was happy and she satisfied Jess or she would have left a long time ago.

"Bertha, where's pa?" he asked.

Surprised, she jumped and turned toward him, then smiled. "Hello, Allan. I didn't hear you come in."

"I'm sorry," he said. "I should have knocked."

"Oh, no," she said quickly. "This is your home, and a man doesn't need to knock when he goes into his home. Why, I haven't seen Jess all morning, but I guess he's in his office. At least that's where he went after breakfast."

"I'll look," he said.

"You'll stay for dinner," she said. "You haven't been here for so long. I'll just have to put on another steak. I've got plenty of everything else."

"Glad to," he said and, turning, crossed the living room and knocked on the office door.

"Come in," Jess bellowed.

He bellowed more often than he spoke in a normal voice, Burke thought as he opened the door. Jess glanced up from his desk and leaned back in his swivel chair. "Well, damn if it ain't my son and heir. You ain't been out here in a coon's age. Must be something big to bring you here today."

"It is," Burke said as he pulled a chair up to the desk and sat down. "I'm asking for help. I just got back from nosing around in Bullhide. Pat Kline tells me the Hall bunch and some more of the North Fork men are fixing to raid Broken Bow and burn it. I can't hold 'em off by myself.

"My uncles and the other old codgers who live in town won't be much help. I don't have a deputy now, so I wondered if you'd let me have some of the Bar B crew to serve as deputies until the Halls make their play."

Jess Burke was a big, clean-shaven man with unruly gray hair and the square jaw that always seemed to fit dominating men. Now he scowled as he laid his gaze on his son's face, hardly blinking as he said, "By God, Al, it's your job to take care of chores like that. When are you going to be big enough to wipe your own nose?"

74

Allan Burke rose, telling himself bitterly that he should have expected that kind of answer. He wheeled and started toward the door, his face red. This was the treatment he had been given all his life, and he had accepted it; the same treatment that had driven Sharon away from home a year ago. In the few seconds that it took him to reach the door, he told himself that he had finally reached the same point that Sharon had. He would never come here again.

"Hold on," Jess shouted. "You don't need to get your tail up. You know the Halls are nothing but a big wind. Old Pat Kline is the same thing. Nothing's gonna come of it."

"Tell Bertha I won't be staying for dinner after all," he said and kept going.

It was not until he was on his horse and halfway to town that he remembered he had not mentioned Lucy to his father. He was surprised at the instinctive way he had reacted to Jess's words. Now, thinking about it, he was glad he hadn't mentioned Lucy. Rebellion was long overdue, but he was free at last. He was his own man. He felt damned good about it. He smiled and put his horse into a gallop, anxious to get off Bar B range.

It was hell to give up the Burke fortune. He had taken a lot of guff over the years just to stay in Jess's favor, and now he would be out in the cold just as Sharon was. At least he thought Jess had changed his will after she had moved to town. The only thing he could do was to go ahead and marry Lucy and say to hell with what his father and his uncles thought. He should have planned on doing that all along.

He turned into the livery stable as soon as he

reached town, thinking he would go to Sharon's Beanery and get dinner. He'd talk to her about paying back
the money he had loaned her, but the stableman hurry-
ing along the runway toward him changed his mind.

"Sheriff, I've got something to tell you," the old man
said shrilly. "I'm worried. You'll probably kick my butt
clean out to the corral, but I couldn't help it. Sharon
went riding this morning with a stranger."

For a moment Burke didn't catch the full import of
what the old man had told him. He said mildly, "I
reckon Sharon knows what she wants to do." Then he
sensed the almost hysterical concern that the liveryman felt, and he asked, "What kind of a stranger?"

"I figure him for a tough hand," the old man said.
"He hit town yesterday, then after supper he had a
set-to in O'Hara's Bar with the Dorn kids and ran 'em
out of town. Today he shows up about ten o'clock and
meets Sharon. Damned if they don't go riding off like
they'd knowed each other all their lives. I tried to talk
her out of it, but you know how bullheaded she
gets."

"I know," Burke said. "What did he look like?"

"He's in his early twenties," the liveryman said.
"Good looking, I guess. Tall. Purty well built. Carries
a gun like he knows how to use it."

"We don't get many like that around here," Burke
said. "Wonder what he's doing in Broken Bow."

"He didn't say," the liveryman said.

"I'm going to the office," Burke said. "Let me know
if they ride in purty soon."

He left the stable and strode to the courthouse,
more disturbed than he wanted to admit. It wasn't like
Sharon to go riding with a strange man. He didn't

know what he'd do if she failed to show up in another hour or two. East Park was a big piece of country for a man to find a girl, but one thing was sure. He wouldn't go back to the Bar B for help.

CHAPTER X

For a long time Sharon sat staring at Mark, then at the ruins of the Cardigan house, and back to Mark again. "I'm shocked," she said finally. "It doesn't seem possible that the Cardigan child who got away would come back twenty years later as a full-grown man."

"Well, he did," Mark said. "My Aunt Kate, she's the woman who took me away and raised me, told me the story, and it pretty well matches the story you just told me."

"What are you going to do now?" she asked. "Are you going gunning for pa?"

He shook his head. "No, but right now I don't know for sure what I'll do."

She made a sweeping gesture that included the entire valley. She said, "By rights this belongs to you. It would only be fair if pa gave it to you."

Mark grinned. "Would he?"

She snorted in derision. "Over his dead body. Why did you come?"

"To see where I was born." He didn't want to tell her about the nightmares. He didn't think anyone who had known him only a few hours would understand. "And to see the kind of men who would murder my father and his brother and would have murdered me and Aunt Kate if they'd had the chance."

She nodded somberly. "You'd think they'd be monsters with horns and tails. Well, they don't have horns and tails, and they aren't really monsters, though they must have been twenty years ago. Once they got all they wanted, they began to mellow. At least my uncles have. Pa isn't as mean as he used to be, but he's just as bullheaded."

"The past is gone, and I can't change it," Mark said, "but it doesn't seem right that three men should continue to prosper and be happy after robbing and murdering as many people as they have."

"Prosper yes," she said. "Happy no. Both Uncle Rodney and Uncle Bob have such bad health they're miserable. I don't know about pa, but I don't think he's very happy. I guess it's a proposition of wanting some things so bad you'll do anything for it, and then after you get it, you find it's not worth what it cost."

He rose. "Let's go back to town. I'm still going to ask your brother for the deputy's job, but I don't know how long I'll stay here. I want to see what your pa and uncles look like, and then maybe I'll head back for home."

"You said I'd have the power of life and death over you if I knew who you were," she said. "You think that if I told pa who you are, he'd try to kill you?"

"I sure do," Mark answered. "He'd have to just in self-defense."

"I won't tell them," she said, "but I think before you leave Converse County, you'll tell them yourself."

"Maybe I will," he said. "You coming?"

"Not yet." She shook her head. "There's one more thing I need to tell you. Sit down."

He dropped down beside her. "You think I can stand any more?"

"I'm not sure you can stand what I'm going to tell you," she said, "but I'm going to tell you anyhow. You see, the story I just told you is the one most people agree on, but it's not the only story. I don't know the truth. I've never asked pa because I don't think he'd tell me, but I've put together scraps of what other people have told me who lived here when it happened.

"Like I said, I was born the year your dad and uncle were killed. Most of the people who live in town now were in the county then, and the fight with the Cardigans was the biggest ruckus and the most exciting thing that ever happened in the county. Folks still talk about it because your dad was an exciting man. I think all the single women were in love with him and some of the married ones, too.

"He was a leader, and I've heard he was organizing the other settlers to fight the Burkes, men like old man Hall and the father of the Dorn boys and others like them. A lot of folks say that was the real reason pa went after him."

Mark rolled a smoke as he listened, thinking that it was good to know that he had an outstanding father, but that fact didn't change anything as far as the Burkes were concerned.

"But that wasn't what I started to tell you," she went on. "There are some other stories about who you are. One says that Marta was pregnant before she left the Bar B to go to your father. That would make us half brother and sister."

"My God," he said softly. "That's hogwash. I don't believe it."

"Neither do I," she said. "It isn't likely that Marta would have left pa if she was pregnant at the time, but it is one of the stories that people tell, probably trying to make a good yarn better. The other one is that your Aunt Kate is really your mother. You see, she was here once before visiting with her sister Marta. She left, then Marta died, and Kate came back to keep house for the Cardigans.

"The point is that nobody around here knows for sure just when you were born. There wasn't any doctor in the county." She stopped and glanced at Mark as if wondering if she should go on. "I can't say nobody knows because there is one old woman we call Grammy Smith who was a midwife and delivered all the babies that were born then. She knows, but she never talks. I've asked her, but she just grins and won't say a word."

"I don't believe that story, either," Mark said. "I don't think Aunt Kate would lie. If she was my mother, she would have accepted me as her son and not her nephew. I mean there was no reason for her to claim I was her nephew if it wasn't true." He stopped and then asked, "You think this Grammy Smith would talk to me?"

"She might," Sharon said. "I take her something to eat three or four times a week. I'll take you with me the next time I go." She rose. "Now are you ready to go?"

"I'm still ready," Mark said.

Neither felt like talking on the ride back. Sharon stared straight ahead, frowning as if caught in the trap of her own thoughts, and Mark, looking to the next few days, wondered if he was smart to stay, or should he start back to Baca County as soon as he talked to Grammy Smith. He dismissed the thought at once. He was going to see the Burke men and maybe, just maybe, he'd tell them who he was.

He might be signing his death warrant if he told them. He couldn't believe that a man as tough as Jess Burke was supposed to be would wait for him to make the first play. If and when Jess tried to kill him, he would have all the excuse he needed to be both judge and executioner. Not that revenge would wipe out what had happened. It was a simple question of justice.

When they reached the edge of town, Mark was struck again by its ugliness, the complete lack of pride, the air of decay that hung over Broken Bow like a miasmic cloud. He burst out, "I don't know how you can stay here, Sharon. It's the worst town I ever saw in my life."

"I agree," she said. "I haven't been to many other towns this size, but I feel the same way you do even after living here as long as I have. It's the reason I take a ride every morning. You see, it's an old-people's town. I guess Allan and I are the only ones living here who might be called young. There's no school for the simple reason that we don't have any children."

"There must be some in the county."

She nodded. "Some of the little ranchers have children, so we've got half a dozen schools, but just try to get enough county money to pay teachers and keep the schoolhouses up."

"People don't have to live in Converse County," he said.

"But it's their homes," she said bitterly. "The Cardigans wouldn't have left. Neither would the Halls nor the Dorns nor any of the others if they hadn't been forced to. I've got plenty of reason to hate my father, and I simply can see no way to improve the situation as long as he's alive and running everything in the county."

They reached the livery stable and reined through the archway. Mark dismounted and gave Sharon a hand. The stableman hurried along the runway, calling to them, "I'm sure glad you're back safe and sound, Miss Sharon."

"And just what did you think would happen to me?" she demanded.

"Well, I . . . I . . ."

"You think I was leaving the country?" she said. "Or that Mark here was going to assault me?"

"I didn't know," the old man sputtered. "Anyhow, your brother wanted to know as soon as you got back."

"Ben Smith, did you tell Al I went riding with a stranger?" she cried.

"I knew he'd want to know about it," the stableman said defensively. "If anything did happen to you, Al would take it out of my hide. You had no business riding off this way with a good-looking jasper like him the first day he's in town."

Anger had been building in Mark from the time the old man had first called to them. He started toward Smith, saying, "I'd like to take a piece of your hide myself."

"Wait." Sharon caught his arm. "I'm mad enough to take the first chunk of his hide. You are an idiot, Ben. An interfering old fool. I never saw a man I couldn't handle."

"You've never seen many men, Miss Sharon," Smith said, "and you sure don't know much about this one."

"Well, you can stop trying to take care of me." She took Mark's hand that was the nearest to her. "Come on. We've got to find Al before he starts after me."

They ran out of the livery stable and turned toward the courthouse. Mark understood more fully now why she hated her father and her uncles and the town, why she was so frantic in her desire to leave Broken Bow. She would never be allowed to live her own life as long as she stayed here, never be free from the smothering protection of people like the weathered old stableman.

He had met this girl only a few hours before, but he had the strange feeling he had known her all of his life. He would not leave Converse County unless she told him to.

CHAPTER XI

Sharon's face was red with anger and she was still gripping Mark's hand when they charged into Al Burke's office. He started to rise from his desk, he opened his mouth to say something, but he didn't get a chance.

Sharon leaned across the desk and, releasing Mark's hand, shook a finger under her brother's nose. "I'm back and I want you to meet Mark Morgan," she cried. "He's the man I went riding with and he's a gentleman. I like him and I don't like Ben Smith telling me where or who or when I can go riding, or your having to know when I get back."

Burke grinned as he dropped back into his chair. "I surrender. I just told Ben to . . ."

"I know what you told him, and I know what you were thinking," she said. "Well, you can just quit thinking it. I'm a grown woman and I'm damned tired of being treated like a ten-year-old."

Burke held up his hands. "I told you I surrendered. After this I won't give a damn what happens to you." He winked at Mark. "Seems like I read somewhere that there's no fury like a mad woman's."

Sharon sniffed. "All right. I'll leave you two alone. Mark came to Broken Bow to see you. Come over and get your dinner after awhile."

She whirled and ran out of the office. Burke got up and extended his hand. "I'm glad to meet you, Morgan. You've made quite an impression on my sister."

Mark shook hands, instinctively liking the man. Somehow he'd picked up the impression that Al Burke was a weakling, a man everybody ran over, a sheriff who had no real sense of duty; but now he changed his mind. Burke's handshake was firm, he looked Mark in the eyes, and he had an intangible air about him of a man who could handle himself. He was a tall man, as tall as Mark and a good deal heavier, and he was handsome in a craggy sort of way.

"I hope I have," Mark said. "She's quite a woman. I've learned a good deal about Converse County since I came here. I admire anyone, man or woman, who can make it on his own."

Burke sat back in his chair. He said, "Sit down and tell me what you mean by that."

Mark drew Abe Gilroy's letter from his pocket and handed it to Burke. "I live in Baca County. I heard you were having trouble keeping deputies, so I'm applying for the job."

Burke took the letter, saying, "You mean you want to be deputy, and you knew I'd had three deputies killed in the last six months?"

"That's right," Mark said.

Burke scanned the letter and laid it on his desk. "Pull up a chair. I don't savvy this. Why do you want the job, knowing the risk you'll take?"

Mark sat down, not sure how to answer the question. Sometime he would tell Al Burke who he was, but not today. "It was pretty quiet in Baca County." He shrugged. "Hell, to be honest, it was the salary."

"I can tell you right now you've got the job if you still want it," Burke said. "I need a good deputy and Gilroy's not a man to lie, so I figure you'll be a good one. But I want you to know before you start that we're in for one hell of a fight. You've seen the people who live here. They're like Ben Smith in the livery stable, old men who are worn down to a nubbin. They won't be much help in a showdown."

"I guess a man figures on doing a certain amount of fighting when he takes a deputy's star," Mark said.

"This is going to be more than average," Burke said. "You've heard of the Halls?" Mark nodded, and Burke went on, "I've never worried about them because we've had a sort of unspoken truce. Actually they aren't wanted in Colorado. Now I get rumors that they're leaving the country, but before they go, they aim to burn the town."

"Why?"

Burke shrugged. "Just out of cussedness, I guess. The old man who runs the family like a king is a mean son of a bitch. Maybe you've heard he was driven out of the park years ago by my father?"

"I've heard," Mark said.

"Well, I guess he's been sitting up there in his canyon brooding about it for twenty years, and now he's decided to get square. I thought I'd get some help from the Bar B crew . . . that's my dad's outfit . . . . but he don't believe the rumors, so that leaves it up to us."

"Looks like I got here just in time for some excitement," Mark said.

"Exactly on time," Burke said. "I wouldn't blame you if you decided to ride back to Baca County."

Mark shook his head. "No, I'm not scared out of it yet, but one thing bothers me. Three deputies murdered, but you're not. Why?"

"I hear that old man Hall put out the word I was to be let alone, and his word is law up there on the North Fork," Burke answered. "I guess it was on account of the truce I mentioned, but now that's off."

"Who killed the deputies?"

"I don't know," Burke said. "If I did, I'd arrest the killer. It could be one of the Dorn boys. They hate all lawmen and that includes me, but they wouldn't go against old man Hall. I understand you had a run-in with the Dorns last night?"

"I did," Mark said. "They were working up to having some fun at my expense. I stopped it before it went that far."

"Then you can expect more trouble with them," Burke said. "They're not the kind to forget."

He opened a desk drawer, took out a star, and tossed it to Mark. "Pin it on. Your pay started this morning. We're both on call if any real trouble starts shaping up. If not, I handle the day shift except on the days when I'm out of town. You're on at night from six to six. There's no town marshall, so most of our work is here in Broken Bow. Normally you stay up till midnight. After that you can go to bed unless there's trouble."

Mark pinned the star on his vest. "I suppose the deputies were shot at night?"

"That's right, and it's been on the nights when the Dorn boys were in town," Burke said. "It doesn't prove anything, but it ought to be a warning."

"Suppose I run them in the next time they show up in town," Mark said. "I mean, even if they haven't done anything. I can always claim they're disturbing the peace. It might discourage them from coming into town. I never cottoned to the idea of making myself a target for killers."

Burke laughed shortly. "Go ahead. I don't like the notion of having to wait until a law is broken before we can arrest the law breaker when you know damned well he's going to break the law."

"Me neither," Mark said.

"When there's anybody in a cell," Burke said, "you sleep here." He jerked a thumb at a cot set against the far wall. "Otherwise you can take a room in the hotel. I'll see you get a cut rate. You can eat at Sharon's place, of course. It's good food."

"I know," Mark said. "I've had a couple of meals there." He rose. "Well, my tapeworm is beginning to howl. You going to eat?"

"Not now," Burke said. "You know, you never did answer my question about what you meant when you said you admired anyone who could make it here on his own."

"I guess it's no secret that the Burke brothers call the tune," Mark said. "From what Sharon told me, I figured Jess Burke didn't want her to leave home and start her own business."

Burke's face lost its amiable expression. He was silent a moment, then he said, "It's no secret about the Burkes calling the tune, but as far as Sharon goes, pa never really put the squeeze on her."

"I want to make one thing clear," Mark said. "I'll arrest a Burke as soon as I would anyone else if he breaks the law. I don't figure that their money and power gives them the right to commit a crime."

"I wouldn't expect you to do anything different," Burke said.

"Then I'm satisfied," Mark said and left the office.

He passed the janitor in the hall who stared at him curiously, then saw the star, and said, "I'll be damned." As usual he was leaning on his broom handle, and that, Mark told himself, was one thing he would change if he had an opportunity.

He went directly to Sharon's Beanery, suddenly realizing he was famished. Sharon was behind the counter and had changed into a blue dress with white lace on the cuffs and collar. It seemed a little ornate for the time and place, and he hoped she had put it on for his benefit.

"I see you're hired," she said.

"I had a letter from the Baca County sheriff," Mark said. "I suppose that helped."

"He'd have hired you anyhow," she said. "What'll you have?"

"Flapjacks with sausage," he said.

"For dinner?"

"Why not? I like 'em."

"Then that's what you're going to get," she said.

When he finished, he shoved his plate back across the counter and dropped a coin beside it. "It's a funny thing, Sharon. I like your brother. Somehow I had the notion he was short on guts or just didn't give a damn about his job. He says there will be big trouble with the Halls, but he didn't seem scared of them."

She stood across the counter from him, motionless, her gaze fixed on his face. "How do you judge a man? A man you know well?"

"I guess you judge a man by what he does," Mark said, "especially in a showdown. But I will bet my life that your brother won't let me down."

"I think I know Al better than anyone else knows him," she said. "Like I told you, he's always been good to me. If he'd just be his own man when it comes to pa's schemes . . ."

"It takes a long time to break a lifetime habit," Mark interrupted, "and sometimes a lot of water has to go over the dam." He grinned. "You've got a hair-trigger temper. I don't think your brother has."

Embarrassed, she said, "I'm sorry about my tantrum, but you don't know . . ."

"I think I do," he said. "I'm looking forward to meeting your father. I think he must have horns and a tail. You just never had the eyes to see."

He left the restaurant, suddenly feeling depressed. Sharon, he knew, hated her father, but whose side would she take when it came to a showdown between them? And there would be a showdown. He thought about Cardigan valley and the ruins of the Cardigan house, and the scene that had come to him so many times in his nightmares, his uncle saying, "Hand the boy up to me," and of the steady beat of hoofs behind them.

Yes, there would be a showdown, all right. It was written in the book.

CHAPTER XII

Mark started to cruise the town at six that evening, exploring every street and alley in Broken Bow. He saw that Sharon had been right about children. There was no indication of them anywhere, and there was no school. He did find a church and stopped to visit with the preacher, Carl Yost, who was working in his garden back of his small house which stood next to the church.

Yost was a man in his sixties, slender, with the gnarled hands of one who had worked hard all his life. He volunteered the information that he had been a farmer in Ohio until about five years before when he had received the call and had come west to find his pastorate.

"I've been here all of these five years, Mr. Morgan," he said, "and I have been disappointed to find that men are not interested in my message. My congregation is composed entirely of women, but folks have to have a minister for marrying and burying, so I feel I am needed here."

"Has there been any violence or disturbance of the peace since you came to Broken Bow?" Mark asked.

Yost shook his head. "No, it's a very peaceful community. I have heard that years ago, when the park was first settled, there was a good deal of violence, but I guess that was not uncommon in ranch communities in those days."

Mark nodded and walked on, thinking that he respected Yost who seemed to have no illusions about his importance in Broken Bow's society. He had not pressed Mark to come to church and had not inquired about the condition of his soul.

By the time Mark had finished, it was dusk. He stepped into O'Hara's Bar, wondering why Converse County needed a deputy and why it would be paying the salary that it was. He ordered a beer, noting that he was alone in the saloon except for O'Hara who didn't appear to have enough business to stay open unless his Saturday trade was enough to give him a profit for the week.

O'Hara was very busy polishing glasses, but he kept watching Mark as if expecting to hear some news from him. When he didn't, he finally blurted, "I see you're wearing the deputy's badge. I guess word got to Al Burke about the way you handled the Dorn boys."

"Maybe it did," Mark said. "O'Hara, were you living here when the Cardigans were killed?"

Startled, O'Hara asked, "Now how did you hear about the Cardigans?"

"They were relatives of mine," Mark said. "I've always been curious about what happened."

"Yeah, I was living here," O'Hara admitted. "As a matter of fact I was bartender in this very saloon before I owned it. Broken Bow was a good town then. It didn't have a single vacant building on Main Street.

There was a lot of little spreads in the park, and on Saturday nights the town was roaring."

"I guess that was before Jess Burke started driving the little fry out of the park," Mark said.

O'Hara hesitated, not sure what was back of the remark, then he said, "That's about it."

"Did you actually see Flint Cardigan killed?" Mark asked. "I've never heard the details. All I know is that Jess Burke killed him because he wanted his ranch."

"It was more than that," O'Hara said. "There was this woman Marta who ran out on Jess and moved in with the Cardigans. Besides that, Flint Cardigan was a troublemaker. He didn't cotton to the way Jess was running things, and he started working up some of the little fry into what they called the East Park Protective Association. He was popular, Flint was, and I always figured that Jess allowed there wouldn't be any peace around here till one of 'em was dead."

"What you're saying is that Jess was plain jealous?"

"That's about it," O'Hara admitted. "Jess was still stuck on Marta even after she left him. I don't guess he ever got over it, but he never jumped Flint with his gun until that day it happened. Flint was too fast for him and he knew it."

"Well, how did it happen?"

O'Hara had been polishing the same glass for the last five minutes. Now he put it down and leaned across the bar. "I've talked enough, my friend. Maybe too much. I don't know why you're so interested in something that happened twenty years ago."

"I told you the Cardigans were relatives of mine," Mark said. "I never did hear the straight of it."

"You may be a deputy today," O'Hara said, "but you won't be on the job no longer than Jess wants you to.

The less you know about ancient history the better. Jess don't like for it to be dug up."

"Now that he's respectable, he don't want to be reminded that he's been a murdering bastard and thief."

O'Hara began backing up away from the bar. "Nobody talks that way in Broken Bow."

Mark leaned across the bar and grabbed a handful of O'Hara's shirt and began to twist it. "I talk that way, and I'm going to dig up a lot of ancient history. Now you're going to tell me how it was."

"I can't," O'Hara muttered. "Jess would kill me if I did."

"No he won't," Mark said. "You're an old man and you're more fat than gristle. I'd be ashamed to hurt you, but that sure as hell is going to happen if you don't finish your story."

O'Hara swallowed, his face turning redder than normal. "You are a tough son of a bitch. Does Al know who he hired?"

"He's going to find out if he doesn't know," Mark said. "Now go ahead."

"Let go."

Mark released his grip, and O'Hara moved farther back so he was out of Mark's reach. He wiped his face with his bandanna, then demanded, "You gonna tell Jess I told you?"

"No. Why should I?"

"I dunno." O'Hara wiped his face again. "Flint was in here by himself. I don't know where Ed was, but he must have been in back somewhere. Jess came in with six or seven of his crew. Rodney and Bob were with him. They were purty good men when they was younger.

"Jess began cussing Flint out, blaming him for Marta

dying the way she'd done. Flint told him to pull. Jess went for his gun, and so did some of his men. I dropped down behind the bar, so I don't know what happened, but it don't make no difference who actually pulled the trigger that beefed Flint. Jess was the one who done it. They started looking for Ed, but he'd got to his horse and cleared out. They caught him later that night just a few miles from town."

"It was murder then," Mark said. "Couldn't be anything else if six or seven men all drew on Flint at the same time."

"You could call it that," O'Hara said, "only nobody does around here." He looked past Mark to the other door, then said softly, "Now we'll see how tough you are, Deputy."

Mark turned to see the three Dorn boys come into the saloon and head for the bar.

CHAPTER XIII

After Mark left the sheriff's office, Al Burke sat in his swivel chair for a long time, his feet on his desk, his thoughts on Lucy and then the Halls and finally his stubborn father. He had never thought he could break off with his father, but he had, and he was relieved, partly because after all these years he was his own man, and partly because he did not have to discuss Lucy with Jess Burke.

He considered riding back to Bullhide in the morning and bringing Lucy to town and marrying her at once, but he had told her he would see her Monday. He'd better let it go at that, he decided. He would bring her back with him on Tuesday.

Before he left town Monday afternoon, he would speak to Carl Yost about marrying them. Lucy would expect him to stall again, and she'd be pleased that he wasn't. He'd tell her he had probably lost the Burke fortune when he'd defied his father, but he was confident that it wouldn't make any difference with her love for him.

There was one thing he had to do today, and he might as well get at it. He rose, clapped his hat on his head, and left the courthouse. He walked to the bank and went in, asking the teller, "Is Uncle Rod in?"

The teller glanced up from his ledger, nodded, and jerked a thumb toward the door marked Private. "Go on in," he said. "He ain't busy."

Al pushed back the gate at the end of the counter and, striding quickly to the office door, opened it and went in. Rodney Burke was dozing in his chair at his desk. The noise of the door opening and closing woke him, and he sat up, gurgling and puffing as he rubbed his eyes.

"Oh, it's you, Al," he said. "Sit down, boy." He motioned to a chair. "Have a cigar."

He flipped the lid of a cigar box back and extended it toward his nephew. Al took a cigar, bit off the end and, thumbing a match to life, fired it as he dropped into a chair.

"You must be at peace with the world," Al said, "sleeping like this in the middle of the day."

Rodney yawned and stretched and rubbed his eyes. He was a fat man with a huge paunch, a placid man who liked the physical comforts of life, peace and order, and the feeling of power that his money gave him. In his early years he had worked hard, but now walking from his house to the bank and back was the most exercise that he had.

"I reckon so," he said. "I don't know of anything that ought to keep me awake at night."

"I do," Al said, thinking that he had never known Rodney to oppose Jess. His uncle simply didn't like to fight, and opposing Jess meant fighting. "That's why I'm here, but first I want to tell you that I've hired a deputy name of Mark Morgan. I suppose you and pa and Uncle Bob will want to pass on him."

"I suppose so," Rodney said. "It's the usual procedure. Is that what's supposed to keep me awake at night?"

"No," Al said, "but the fact that I will keep Morgan as deputy no matter what you three say might."

"The hell." Rodney pushed his chair back and put his hands on his desk. "Now just what does that mean?"

"It means I'm rebelling," Al said. "Through all the time I was growing up and while I've been sheriff, I've agreed to everything you three say, which means what pa says because you and Uncle Bob never give pa any back talk."

"No, I reckon we don't," Rodney agreed. "It always seems that Jess is the leader of the family. He knows what to do. As a matter of fact we wouldn't be where we are now without Jess. Maybe it's habit, but I see no reason not to go along with what he says."

Al thought of a number of things he could say at that point, as to whether Rodney still agreed to robbery and murder which had been the route the Burkes had taken to reach the place they now occupied.

He had never understood how Rodney, a good-natured, law-abiding man, could have taken part in Jess's violent actions twenty years ago; but it was all history now, and he saw no reason to bring it up.

"You won't go along with what he says about one thing," Al said, "and you'll argue like hell with pa, both you and Uncle Bob. I picked up a rumor that the Halls are planning to raid and burn Broken Bow. I asked pa for some of the Bar B crew to protect the town, and he said that was my job. That's one reason I'm glad this man Morgan showed up when he did. He seems to be competent, and we sure as hell will need him."

Rodney's face had turned pale. "You sure about this?"

Al shook his head. "No way to be sure about it till they get here. I heard it from Pat Kline. The Halls had been drinking in his bar and got to talking. Old man Hall said they were planning a big job in Wyoming, and they'd be leaving the North Fork in a few days and he was going to get square with the Burkes before he left. Burning Broken Bow was his way of doing it."

Rodney was silent for a time. He was breathing hard and, taking a handkerchief from his pocket, he wiped his face. Finally he said, "Well, by God, you know how to keep a man awake at night all right." He wiped his face again. "Why won't Jess let you have the men?"

"You know how damned arrogant he is," Al said. "He won't believe the Halls or anyone else has the guts to tackle the Burkes, so he figures it's all hogwash, that the Halls are just big talkers."

"We can't sit here and let 'em surprise us," Rodney said. "It might be true. You'd better get out to the Bar B and tell Jess about your new deputy. That'll bring him into town, and Bob and me will try to talk some sense into him."

Al shook his head. "I'm not going to the Bar B for anything, and I never will unless it's a matter of sitting beside pa's bed while he's dying. I said I'm rebelling. He's told me too many times to wipe my own nose, and from now on I'm going to."

"How's he going to know about your deputy?" Rodney asked, "and how are Bob and me going to get a chance to talk to him?"

"You or Uncle Bob will go to the Bar B and tell

him," Al said. "It's as much to your interest to protect this no-good town as it is mine." He rose. "Let me know if pa comes in. If he does, I'll fetch Morgan to the meeting, but don't expect it to be a pleasant one."

"This is not to my liking," Rodney said as if it were an impossible task. "Bob's health is too bad for him to leave town, and I haven't been in a buggy for a year."

"Then send somebody else," Al said. "Send pa a note."

"Maybe I'll do that," Rodney said, wiping his face again. "What brought this rebellion on, boy? It's not like you."

Al laughed shortly. "No, it's not, but I will tell you one thing. I feel proud of myself for doing something I should have done a long time ago." He paused, thinking that if it hadn't been for Lucy, he probably wouldn't have made the break now. But he didn't want to talk to Rodney about the girl, so he merely said, "I guess it was just a proposition of getting my bellyful of taking pa's orders."

He wheeled and left the office, grinning as he thought of Rodney's reluctance to confront Jess about anything. Rodney was not just a peaceful man. He was a cowardly man. So was Bob Burke. So was he. Or had been. But it was different now. Loving Lucy had been partly responsible for his change, but it was more than that. He decided that more than anything else it was the gut realization that he owed something to himself, to his job, and, of course, to Lucy, that had made a man out of him, and now, by God, he was; and he was proud of it.

There was nothing for him to do at the courthouse, so he went home, thinking for the first time how it would be to have Lucy here. He stopped in the doorway and looked around, realizing that he couldn't bring her here with the house as dirty as this. The place was a boar's nest. He didn't know of anyone he could hire to clean, so he'd have to do it himself. The house was not large; one bedroom, one living room, and a very small kitchen, but it would have to do.

He worked the rest of the afternoon and into the evening, telling himself he'd have Sharon come over before he brought Lucy to Broken Bow. She could do some of the little things he would overlook, but would help a woman feel at home.

He didn't realize until nearly sundown that he was hungry, that he hadn't eaten since morning. He threw the dirty water out through the back door, leaned the mop handle against the wall of the kitchen, and slapped his hat on his head.

Lucy always kept the Bullhide Inn immaculate. He'd be entering a whole new life, he told himself. He'd have to wipe his feet every time he came into the house, then he thought of the cold winter nights he'd slept by himself, and the sourness fled. The new life had to be better than the old.

When he sat down at the counter in Sharon's Beanery, she said, "Well, I thought you had gone on a fast."

"I wasn't hungry at noon," he said, "and this afternoon I got busy cleaning my house up and I forgot I was hungry."

"You?" She stared at him in feigned astonishment. "Clean your place up and forget to eat? Brother, you have gone loco. I can't remember when you used a broom or a mop in your house or forgot to eat when it was mealtime."

"Go put my steak on," he said, "and I'll tell you about it."

Sharon went back into the kitchen. When she returned, she said, "I guess you liked my friend Mark. I see he's wearing a star."

"He'll do," Burke said, too intent on his problems to discuss Mark Morgan. "Sharon, I'm going to marry Lucy Kline."

This time she was honestly amazed. Finally she said, "I don't believe it, Al. Pa would never stand for you marrying a breed girl."

"Pa won't have anything to do with it," he said. "I don't give a damn what he thinks. I finally did what you did a year ago, and I feel good about it. I bowed and scraped around him all my life just because I didn't want to lose my share of the Burke money, but hell, he may outlive me. I rode away from the Bar B this morning, and I'm never going back."

"Are you serious?"

"Oh, I'm serious, all right," he said. "I'm so serious that I told Uncle Rodney this afternoon to get word to pa himself about me hiring a new deputy if they want a conference with us."

"Suppose pa doesn't like Mark?"

"I don't give a damn about that either," he said. "Morgan stays hired as long as I'm sheriff."

She walked around the counter and hugged and kissed him. She said, "I'm glad, Al. I'm proud of you."

"I'm a little proud of myself," he said sheepishly. "Now I'm wondering why I didn't do it a long time ago. Oh, after I finish cleaning and painting the house, I'd like for you to come by and look it over. I'll bring her back with me next Tuesday."

"Of course I will," she said. "Oh, Al, I can't tell you

who Mark really is, but I'm going to ask him to tell you himself. You'll be surprised."

Later, when he left the restaurant, he saw three men go into O'Hara's Bar. The light was thin, but he was sure they were the Dorn boys. He paused, wondering if Morgan was in the bar and if he should give his deputy a hand. He decided not and walked on to his house. Morgan would have to handle his own problems.

Then he thought about Sharon saying she couldn't tell him who Morgan was. Well, it probably didn't make any difference, and his thoughts turned to Lucy. Maybe he was crazy to wait until next week to marry her. Then he remembered the Halls' threat to burn the town. He didn't want her here if that happened. He might have to wait longer than a week, but now that he'd made up his mind, he thought he couldn't wait.

CHAPTER XIV

The instant Mark saw the Dorn boys, he knew he had to move fast, that they were here for only one purpose, that he had to make his play before they decided how to take him. His first impulse was to order them out of Broken Bow, but he remembered that Al Burke suspected them of killing the three deputies. If he forced them to leave town, they would only come back later in the night and dry-gulch him. He had one alternative: to jail them.

He moved toward them, his gun in his hand. They appeared to ignore him, but he sensed they were aware of every move he made. When he was no more than a step from the youngest Dorn, he said, "Loosen your gun belts and lay them on the bar. When you leave town, you can get them back from O'Hara."

"What are you going to do?" the youngest one demanded.

"I'm going to jail you," Mark said. "In case you hadn't noticed, I'm the new deputy."

"What the hell have we done to be jailed for?" the one at the far end demanded. "We come in peaceable for a drink, and now you say you're jailing us. Why?"

"Last night you promised to kill me," Mark answered. "That's enough to hold you on. Besides, I've heard rumors that you're the ones who murdered three deputies in the last six months. I don't aim to be a pigeon for you. You can't shoot me when you're in jail. Now do what I told you."

For a moment they stood as if frozen, then the youngest one yanked his knife from its scabbard and whirled toward Mark. He had expected some kind of move but not with a knife. He batted Dorn's hand to one side and swung his gun in a short, downward blow that caught the young outlaw on top of the head. He sagged, his knife dropping from his hand. Mark put an arm around him and kept him from falling, his gun lined on the other two.

"If either one of you makes a stupid move like that," Mark said, "you'll get a slug in your brisket. Your time's run out. Lay your gun belts on the bar."

They obeyed, sullen faced, neither saying a word. "Now you," Mark nodded at the one who stood in the middle, "take your brother's gun and lay it on the bar, then keep him on his feet and get out of here."

The youngest Dorn wasn't unconscious, but he was close to it. His brother held him upright with one arm as he lifted his gun from the holster with the other hand and laid it on the bar. They turned toward the batwings, walking slowly, Mark two steps behind them.

As they stepped onto the boardwalk, Mark said, "In the middle of the street, then turn right."

There was no argument left in them. One man across the street who was about to go into Sharon's Beanery stopped and watched, but he made no effort to interfere. The four of them trudged through the dust until they reached the courthouse, then Mark said, "Turn right again. Go the length of the hall when you get inside, and keep going into the jail."

If they scattered on him, he'd have one hell of a time rounding them up. He might hit one as they ran, but in the darkening twilight even that was unlikely. It was proof of their innate cowardice that they didn't try. They were, Mark told himself, the kind who would shoot a lawman in the back. Not many men would do that, a fact that underlined Al Burke's suspicions that they were the deputy killers.

They tromped across the courthouse yard, climbed the steps, and moved on down the long hall to the sheriff's office. The interior of the courthouse was dark except for one bracket lamp on the wall. Again Mark was afraid that they would scatter. There were enough black corners here to hide in so that he couldn't shoot with any certainty of hitting one of them. If he tried to hunt them down, one could jump him from the darkness and give all three a chance to gang up on him.

They failed to take advantage of their opportunity. They didn't stop until they reached the jail wall on the far side of the sheriff's office, giving Mark a chance to light the lamp that was on the desk. He moved toward them, motioning for them to step aside. By the lamplight he could see the expressions of feral hatred that were on their faces, reminding him of dogs he had seen, their lips curled back in vicious snarls, wanting to attack but lacking the courage to do it.

He swung the metal door open, motioning for them to go into the large cell on the left, and closed and locked the cell door. The youngest one had recovered enough to stand by himself. He held a hand to his head as he said, "You bastard! You can't keep us here forever. I promised last night to kill you, and by God, now I know I will."

Mark said nothing as one of his brothers yelled, "How long are you fixing to keep us in here?"

He didn't answer. He closed the door that opened into the jail corridor and sat down at his desk, suddenly weak. It had been a fool thing to do by himself. He should have gone after Burke. Together it would have been an easy task; alone it was foolhardy.

He didn't look forward to spending the night on the cot. Already the Dorn smell was pervading the office. It had been Burke's instructions to stay here when there was anyone in the jail, but he took enough time to move the Dorns' horses to the livery stable, then returned to the sheriff's office.

He lay down on the cot, but he found it impossible to sleep. Finally he thought to hell with his orders and spent the rest of the night in his hotel room. He rose at dawn and was in the office when Al Burke came in.

"What's that stink?" Burke asked.

"The Dorn boys," Mark said. "I locked 'em up."

"The hell you did," Burke said and grinned. "I saw 'em go into O'Hara's Bar and wondered if you were in there."

"I was," Mark said, "and I figured I didn't dare let 'em scatter and get out of my sight or I'd be your fourth dead deputy, so I escorted 'em to a cell."

"You should have come after me," Burke said. "It was a damn fool trick to handle it by yourself. I thought about coming over to see if you were in the saloon but figured you'd want to handle 'em yourself. Hell, I didn't think about you jailing 'em."

"No knowing where they would have been if I'd gone after you," Mark said. "Anyhow, it's done now. I'm ready to let 'em out if it's all right with you."

"Sure," Burke said. "We don't have nothing to hold 'em on."

Mark unlocked the door of their cell. He said, "Your horses are in the livery stable. Get out of town and stay out."

"We're getting out of town," one of them said, "but we ain't staying out. You can count on that."

They tramped down the hall, none of them looking back. Burke stared at them until they were out of the courthouse, then he said, "They'll be back, all right, only next time you won't see 'em."

"Maybe I'll smell 'em," Mark said and left the office.

He returned to his room, slept until noon, then crossed the street to Sharon's Beanery. Sharon was there as he hoped she would be. He said, "Good morning. I was afraid you'd be gone on your daily ride."

"Good morning, Deputy," she said, smiling. "I've had my ride and I'm back for the day. I'm usually here to serve dinner. Jody, she's the woman who helps me, stays if I'm late getting here or too tired to work. What'll it be this morning?"

"Breakfast for me," he said. "Ham and eggs." She started toward the kitchen but stopped when he called, "Wait. I've got something to say and I want to say it before someone comes in."

"You'd better mean it," she said.

"Oh, I mean it," he said. "There are some things a man never joshes about and this is one. That story you were telling me, about us maybe being half-sister and brother. I don't feel like a brother to you, and I want to lay that story to rest. When can we go see the old lady you were talking about?"

"I know exactly what you're talking about," she said. "I don't feel sisterly toward you either. We'll see her tomorrow morning when I take some food to her."

She whirled away from him and ran into the kitchen. He rolled a smoke, telling himself that he had never met a girl like her. She was far ahead of the girls like Cherry he had known in Springfield. Still it was the height of stupidity to hope there could ever be anything between them.

CHAPTER XV

Old man Hall sat on his porch and stared down the canyon that led to the North Fork. He spent most of his days this way, staring and dreaming, while his boys were hunting. His house was made of logs, a long, low structure. He had built it so each boy would have a room of his own. It had served his family well, and now after twenty years it was as tight as the day he had finished building it.

Below the house the canyon walls were very close, with a trickle of water running swiftly along the bottom. He had chosen this location because it would be easy to defend in case the law came after him, but it never had. Above the house the canyon widened into a valley that was large enough to furnish grass for his horses and milk cow and give his wife a garden space.

He had seen Bullhide boom and die, and he was glad it was dead. He was a man who liked solitude, and he had plenty of that. Besides he'd had three boys to raise. He'd taught them how to fight and hunt and drink, but he hated the gamblers and whores who flocked to mining camps, and he was glad to see them go. He didn't want his boys to get a disease from whores, and if there was any spare money, he wanted it laid away in the cache under the floor and not thrown away in a crooked poker game.

He knocked his pipe out on his heel and called, "Ma, fetch me a cup of coffee."

He was a big man, with long white hair and a white beard. The years had brought a slight stoop to his shoulders, but his mind was as sharp as ever, his physical strength nearly as great as when he'd left East Park.

His wife brought him the coffee and stood for a moment beside him. She said, "I don't want to leave here. We're safe and we're happy. I don't see no reason to leave."

She had been a good wife, obedient and hard working. Now he looked at her, wondering why she was rebelling after all this time. He said, "We've saved enough to go south. I've sat here for twenty years dreaming about living where it's warm. Seems to me the winters are getting colder and the snow is getting deeper and my rheumatism is getting worse."

"If we've saved enough to go south,' she said, "why are you planning this last holdup? Every time you leave here, I die until I see you and the boys riding back up the canyon. You've been lucky so far. Why keep on taking risks?"

"We ain't just been lucky," he said irritably. "We've been careful and we're good. I figure this will work out the same. I'll hear by the first of the week what day the money is coming through. You'll stay overnight in Laramie and then take the train to Salt Lake City and you'll wait for us there. I don't figure on taking any risks."

She looked down at him for a full minute, tears running down her cheeks. "I've got a bad feeling about this," she said, "but you're a stubborn man. You'll never change and you'll never listen."

She whirled and stomped back into the house. He grinned and finished his coffee. Just one more job and then twenty years of holding up trains and banks and stagecoaches would be over. Oh, they had enough to go south on, but there would be fifty thousand dollars coming through on the Union Pacific within a week. That meant the difference between a life of luxury and one of pinching pennies. He'd never known luxury. His wife had never had a servant, but she'd have a maid when they got to Mexico.

Along with the dream of spending his last years in a warm country, he'd had another dream, a dream that had eased the ulcer that had eaten on him for the full twenty years. He'd tucked his tail and run when the Burkes told him to sell out to them or he'd wind up dead. At first he thought Jess was just talking, but after the Cardigans' killing, he knew it was more than talk.

At the time the boys had been children. He would have fought if he'd had any chance of winning, but he was always a man who measured the odds. The Cardigans had tried to organize the small ranchers against the Burkes and they might have succeeded if they had lived, but no one else had the capacity for leadership they'd had. He knew that none of his neighbors would stand and fight, so he would have been alone against the three Burkes and the Bar B crew of hard cases.

Well, he hadn't gone many miles, he reflected. He'd holed up here, built his house with the pittance Jess

Burke had paid him for his place in East Park, and he'd lived by hunting and panning gold on the North Fork. When the boys were old enough to handle their end of things, he'd started out on the owl-hoot trail and he'd done well.

"Keep your nose clean in Colorado," he'd told his boys, "and the law in Broken Bow ain't gonna get real curious about you."

It had worked that way. Of course they had never been identified. There had been some ugly rumors about them, largely based on coincidence. It seemed that while they were gone, a bank in Montana would be held up or a train in Wyoming derailed and robbed.

If the sheriff in Broken Bow asked questions, the Halls said that they were gone after cattle. He had a brand and ran a shirttailful of cows in the valley above the house, but the cattle business had never been more than a blind to cover his more profitable activities. After Al Burke had pinned on the star, Hall hadn't even been questioned.

Now this second dream was about to be fulfilled. Twenty years of power and money had been harder on the Burkes than poverty had been on the Halls. Bob was sick, consumption some said. He was thin and weak and coughed blood. He had another year of life according to the talk in Broken Bow. Rodney had gone to fat and seldom did any work harder than shaving and walking to the bank.

Jess? Well, there was a man. The old man had to admit it. When he'd left East Park, Jess Burke had been the meanest and toughest son of a bitch Hall had ever run into. He hadn't gone to pot, but he had mellowed. Still he was probably as bullheaded and mean tempered as ever. It was just that he hadn't had to fight anyone for a long time. He was thinking that nobody would be stupid enough or have enough guts to tackle the Burkes.

The old man laughed aloud as he filled and lighted his pipe. He'd see about who had the guts. He'd wait until he heard when the money was due, then he'd hit the Burkes and wipe them out before he left Colorado. He'd have the Dorn boys along with his sons, and he'd get two or three more among the settlers on the North Fork, men who had reason to hate the Burkes and would be glad for a chance to pick up a few hundred dollars.

The Dorn boys were crazy, but they obeyed him. Everybody on the North Fork obeyed him. This was something he had established when he first settled on the North Fork, and in those days even the toughs in Bullhide had not crossed him.

He was startled to hear horses in the canyon. He didn't like visitors, and everyone was aware of that. No one knew he had a fortune buried under the house, but someone might suspect and he didn't want anyone nosing around here.

"Someone's coming, ma," he called.

She was there in a matter of seconds, handing him his rifle, then moving back into the house where she stood just inside the door, a Winchester in her hands.

A moment later he said, "Hell, it's just the Dorns." He cursed for a full minute, then demanded, "What in hell do you suppose brought 'em up here? They know better."

"Go find out and send 'em back," his wife said.

"I will," Hall said as he rose. "By God, I will."

He stepped off the porch, watching the three Dorns spur their lathered horses up the trail. They knew better than to treat horses that way, too. They were crazy, but not that crazy.

They pulled up in front of him, but before he got out a word, the youngest Dorn, Bud, bellowed, "We want to go with you when you leave Colorado. But before you go, we want you to help us rub out a new deputy that Burke's got in Broken Bow."

Hall didn't say what he intended to say. This was something new, the Dorn boys asking for help to rub out a deputy. He said, "Well now, I figured you all were experts on rubbing out deputies. How come you need my help?"

"This one's a tough son of a bitch," Bud said. "He got the drop on us and threw us into the calaboose. We've been in his lousy jug all night."

They looked as if they had been crying. In all the years he had watched them grow up, he had never known one of them to cry about anything. Now he understood. They were more than angry. They were out of their heads with fury. Bud wiped a sleeve across his eyes and blinked, the corners of his mouth working. They were completely undisciplined, growing up and answering to no one, and now to have been jailed overnight was enough to make them crazier than ever.

"I'm sorry, boys," he said. "You'll have to stomp your own snakes."

"All right, we can do it," Bud said, "but when you go, take us with you. You can use three more guns and we can use some dinero. We'll come back and finish this goddamned deputy ourselves."

"Before we leave Colorado," Hall said, "we'll go into Broken Bow with you. I've got a few snakes to stomp myself, and I can use three more guns. But you ain't going with us when we leave the state."

"What's the matter with us?" the oldest Dorn demanded. "Ain't we good enough to side you? You think we ain't got the guts to do what you ask?"

Hall told himself he was on tricky ground. He needed the Dorns when he raided Broken Bow, but taking them into Wyoming would be suicide. The danger was that if he made them any madder, he'd lose them.

"It ain't that, Sid," he said. "It's just that the four of us have operated together for so long that we know what to do. Anybody else with us would just ball us up." He turned back to his house, calling over his shoulder, "I'll let you know when we're ready to hit Broken Bow."

"We'll show you what we can do," Bud bawled. "By God, you can't treat us this way. We don't need you."

They wheeled their horses and roared back down the canyon. He turned and watched them go, vaguely uneasy. Maybe he had lost them. Then he shrugged and turned again to his house. He'd get along without them if he had to. They were too crazy to be dependable anyway.

CHAPTER XVI

When Mark stepped into Sharon's Beanery on Thursday morning, he found Jody behind the counter. She said, "Good morning, Deputy. What are you having for breakfast?"

"Flapjacks," he said. "Sharon here?"

Jody jerked her head toward the back of the building. "She'll be with you in a minute. She's getting some food ready for Grammy Smith."

Jody brought his flapjacks a few minutes later. He was finished when Sharon came out of the back, a box in her hand. She said, "Good morning, Mark. You ready for Grammy?"

"I'm ready," he said. "I've been ready ever since you told me about her."

She nodded, her face grave. She was as nervous about this meeting as he was, he thought. He was pleased to think that the notion they were half-brother and sister had no more appeal to her than it did to him.

He paid for his meal and slid off the stool. "I'll be back before dinner time," Sharon said to Jody.

They went into the street together, Sharon reaching

out and taking his hand. She said, "I think I know how you feel. You don't know which would be worse, for us to be brother and sister or for Jess Burke to be your father."

"Both are crazy ideas," he said, "and I won't consider either one. I won't believe Grammy Smith if she says they're true."

She sighed. "I'm afraid we'll have to."

They turned down a side street. When they reached the middle of the block, Sharon said, "It's the next house. Don't get angry if she won't talk. There's some days when she's as sharp as anybody in Converse County, but there are other days when her mind is dull. She acts like she doesn't hear you when you ask a question. Doc Jones says old people are often that way. Just bad days and good days."

"Well then," he said, "I guess we'll have to come back if we hit her on a bad day."

Sharon opened the gate that led through a rickety picket fence. "She used to have the best-kept yard in town," she said, "but she can't take care of it any more, and she can't afford to hire anyone. It's her brother who runs the livery stable, but I guess he has all he can do without coming up here and looking after Grammy."

Her house was a small white frame building that needed paint. Half of the pickets were gone from the fence. The yard was grown up with weeds, and one step leading to the porch was broken. Sharon nudged Mark as she approached the house, nodding at the broken step.

Grammy Smith was sitting in her rocker, a tiny wisp of a woman who looked as if she weighed less than ninety pounds. Her hair was white, her face deeply carved by wrinkles, and the backs of her hands were covered by dark, brown splotches. She sat staring across the yard at some distant point and probably seeing nothing, Mark thought.

She didn't seem to be aware of anyone's approach until Sharon said loudly, "Good morning, Grammy."

The old woman's face suddenly brightened as she turned toward Sharon. "Is that you, girl?" she asked. "Yes, of course it's you, and you brought me something to eat, didn't you?"

"I certainly did," Sharon said. "I've got a lemon pie, some biscuits, and a piece of roast beef."

"Thank you," Grammy said. "I guess I'd starve to death if it wasn't for you." Only then was she aware that someone was with Sharon. She said as if irritated, "Who's that with you? I hope it isn't another Burke you found somewhere. I never seen a Burke except you who didn't need shooting."

"Now Grammy," Sharon said, "you don't think Allan is so bad, do you?"

"No, he ain't so bad," Grammy admitted. "Not as bad as them two uncles of yours and your daddy. Now you going to tell me who this is?"

"I want you to meet Mark Morgan, Grammy," Sharon said. "He's Allan's new deputy."

Grammy held out her clawlike hand. Mark was surprised to find that her grip was firm. "You're big enough," she said, "and I hope you're honest. Of course deputies don't live long in Converse County. I guess you know that."

"I've heard about it," he said. "I'm going to keep my eyes open."

"You'd better." She sighed. "I don't know what things are coming to, with three deputies killed in the last six months. I suppose it was the Halls. I used to know the Halls. That was in the days before the Burkes started running the county. Good people, both of 'em."

She sighed again. "Funny thing, Mr. Morgan. I can remember things that happened twenty years ago better'n I can remember what happened yesterday. Sometimes I even forget to eat. Ain't that terrible?"

Sharon had slipped inside and had left the box of food on the kitchen table. She returned in time to hear Grammy say she could remember things that happened twenty years ago better than what had happened yesterday. She said, "That's why Mr. Morgan came with me today, Grammy. We were riding together the other day and crossed Cardigan valley. I was telling him about the Cardigans. You remember Flint, don't you?"

"Yes indeed," Grammy said. "I remember Flint Cardigan. He was a man you never forget."

"We were talking about Kate Morgan and the little boy she had with her when she left," Sharon said. "You know there was some gossip about the boy being my father's child and . . ."

"Land sakes, Sharon," Grammy cried. "That's poppycock. All poppycock. They just love to talk, folks do. But it was kind of strange, Marta leaving your pa the way she did and moving in with the Cardigans. But the boy was Flint's all right."

"There was even some talk that the baby was really Kate's," Sharon said.

"Oh, my God," Grammy said in disgust. "That's even worse. I was there when the baby was born. I ought to know. He was Marta's baby. I brought him into the world, and I took care of him till Kate got here. It makes me mad, plain old mad for folks who don't know nothing about things to make up lies like that. Why don't they come to me and ask? I'm the only one who knows."

Mark was watching the old woman closely. He was relieved to hear what she'd just said, but there was still a question in his mind that had to be asked. He said, "How can you be so sure the baby was Flint's?"

"I just know, young man," she said tartly. "You don't need to ask me how I know when I know."

"There must be something that let's you know," Sharon said.

"Of course there is," Grammy snapped. "He looked just like Flint. I saw that the day he was born. Besides, it takes nine months to make a baby, and Marta was married to Flint for ten months before the baby came. She couldn't have been pregnant when she got there."

Grammy paused and stared at Mark, then she motioned for him to come closer. "I don't see real good at a distance, young man, but I see all right up close. I was thinking that you look a little like Flint, about the same size and all."

She nodded and cackled when his face was close enough for her to see it clearly. "Yes indeed, you do look like Flint. He was a handsome man, Flint Cardigan was. I don't blame Marta for leaving Jess Burke. I knew the Cardigan boys before we ever came to East Park. In those days there wasn't any doctor closer'n Laramie or Fort Collins or Grand Lake. Flint, he figured there ought to be somebody here in the park who could deliver babies and set broken bones, so when they drove their cattle down from the Laramie plains, I just came along."

She took a long breath, her gaze on that distant point again. "I was a nurse in Laramie, you know. Flint, he had a broken leg from getting throwed off a horse. I was an old woman even then, but Flint liked me. I done a good job nursing him when he was laid up, and he thought I'd make a living here in the park. I did, too, as long as I was able to get around. Even Doc Jones says I done a good job."

Suddenly a thought seemed to prod Grammy's mind and she leaned forward in her chair, her hands gripping the arms of the rocker. "Just why are you so interested in the Cardigans, young man?"

He didn't want to tell her the truth, but he wasn't sure that she hadn't guessed. He backed away, saying, "I talked to Kate Morgan in Springfield. She's a relative of mine. She told me about the Cardigans, and after I got here, I was curious about them."

"With you looking like Flint . . ." Grammy began.

"I've got to go, Grammy," Sharon said. "I told Jody I'd be back to take over. She had some things to do at home."

"You go right ahead," Grammy said and waggled a forefinger at Mark. "When you see Kate again, you tell her you seen Grammy Smith when you were here. She'll remember me."

"I'll tell her," Mark promised.

"I'll see you in a day or two," Sharon said and stepped off the porch, Mark following.

When they were on the boardwalk and headed back toward Main Street, Sharon asked, "Satisfied?"

"Sure I am," he said. "I knew the truth all the time." He laughed shortly. "I don't know if she made it up about me looking like Flint Cardigan, but I sure figured she was guessing the truth."

123

"Of course she did," Sharon said. "But by tomorrow she'll have forgotten you were even there, so it's nothing to worry about." She paused, glancing at him, then said, "Mark, I want you to come to supper tonight at six. I don't mean in the restaurant but back in my room. I'm going to have Allan there, too. I want you to tell him who you are."

"Any particular reason?"

She hesitated, then asked, "You going to tell pa?"

"Yes, I am," Mark said. "I'm not sure just when, but I'll tell him."

"Allan will back you up when you do," she said, "He's a changed man. I didn't think he ever would be. Anyhow, he ought to know before he hears it from pa or hears you tell pa."

"All right, I'll tell him," Mark said.

He would not tell them about the nightmares, he thought. He was sure they were gone forever, and now, with a strange peace of mind he had never known before, they were not as real or as terrifying as they had been for so long. The nightmare that was coming to a climax here in Converse County seemed far more real.

CHAPTER XVII

When Mark stepped into the restaurant that evening at six, Jody told him to go on back through the kitchen to Sharon's room. He walked along the counter and on through the kitchen that was filled with a combination of good smells and went into the next room. Sharon was setting the table. She looked up and smiled.

"You're right on time," she said.

"I thought I'd better get here and eat and get back to my job," Mark said. "Al told me I go on duty at six."

"You think there's that much crime in Converse County?" she asked.

"I guess Al thinks so," he answered, "especially after the Halls made their threats."

"Well, if you're needed, we'll soon know." Sharon motioned to a rocker. "Sit down. Supper is just about ready, and Al is never late for a meal."

Mark dropped into the chair and looked around. The room was a combination bedroom, dining room, and living room. The bed that was neatly covered by a red and white afghan was pushed against the far wall. Several pictures were on the wall, all paintings of local scenes that Mark recognized. He guessed they had been done by some itinerant painter who had more time than money and had talked Sharon into taking them for his meals.

A rocker was the only chair in the room except for the dining-room chairs that were set around the table. A walnut claw-footed stand stood in the center of the room. It held two lamps, so Mark guessed that was where Sharon sat when she read. He rose and walked to a small bookcase. Getting down on his knees, he examined the books. They were mostly English novels along with some of Mark Twain's books and several volumes of Longfellow's, Whittier's, and Lowell's poetry.

Sharon returned to the room with a platter of sliced roast. She said, "Take any of those you want, Mark, if you need something to read."

He straightened up. "I've never done much reading. Aunt Kate wasn't a reader, so I have never been around books."

"Well, did any of those look interesting?"

"I think I'd like to try one of Twain's," he said. "*Tom Sawyer* maybe. Twain ought to be a good writer, having the same first name I have."

She nodded. "He is a good writer. Take it when you leave. I've read it at least four times, and I always enjoy it. You'll have plenty of time to read if you keep the deputy job. Right now I'd like to know where that brother of mine is. Oh, there he comes. Speak of the devil."

"What do you mean, speak of the devil?" Al Burke asked as he came into the room. "I heard what you said."

"It's the first time I ever knew you to be late for a meal," Sharon said.

"I've been looking around," he said. "You know, in all the time I've been sheriff, I have never before had a situation I didn't know how to handle. I sure don't know what to do about this Hall business. Pa might be right that it's just a big wind, but I can't count on it. If they do raid the town, how can two of us stop 'em?"

"You're not going to do it before supper. It's all on." Sharon motioned to one chair. "Sit there, Mark. And Al, you sit here."

The meal was a good one, as Mark had known it would be. Besides the roast Sharon served mashed potatoes, gravy, biscuits, and honey. When they finished, she brought coffee and a lemon pie which she cut into quarters.

"I'm glad Grammy didn't get all the lemon pie," Mark said. "You had my mouth watering when you told her what you'd brought her."

"I made two," Sharon said. "Now then, while we're eating dessert, I want you to tell Al what your real name is."

Mark picked up his coffee cup and drank. Burke looked at him questioningly. Mark said, "I've been thinking about what you said this morning and I . . ."

"Tell him," Sharon said more sharply than he had ever heard her speak before. "Trust me, Mark. I know it is better for all of us if Al knows."

Her brusqueness irritated him. He suspected this was a quality she had inherited from Jess Burke. Then he shrugged, realizing she knew her brother better than he did, so he nodded.

"All right," he said. "My real name is Mark Cardigan.

I'm the boy that Kate Morgan saved the night Flint and Ed Cardigan were murdered."

Al Burke had a bite of lemon pie halfway to his mouth. It remained that way for a full ten seconds, his mouth open, his eyes showing shock. Slowly he lowered his fork to his plate and shook his head.

"I'll be damned," he said softly. "I surely will."

Sharon giggled. "Al, I haven't seen you that confused since you got bucked off old Dynamite and your head was addled for an hour or two. I guess I looked and felt the same way when he told me. It doesn't seem possible that someone out of the past could show up here in Converse County like this."

"Why are you here?" Burke asked. "You come back to claim Cardigan valley?"

"No," Mark said. "Not now at least. I guess I just had to see where I was born and what kind of men it took to kill my father and uncle and who wanted to kill me." He lifted his cup of coffee, then remained motionless for a moment before he drank. "I had to come, Al. It was a chapter in my life I had to know more about."

He set the coffee cup down. Someday he would tell them both about his nightmares, but not now. He wasn't sure why he felt that way except that he was still certain that anyone who had not had the experience he'd had with nightmares for so many years could understand what they had done to him.

Burke finished his lemon pie before he said anything more. Then he leaned back in his chair, his anxious gaze on Mark. He asked, "What are you fixing to do? Are you going gunning for pa?"

"Not unless he forces it," Mark answered.

"Tomorrow afternoon we show up before my uncles

and pa," Burke said. "We let them see who I hired for my deputy. I want you to understand now, Mark, that no matter what they say or do, you are still my deputy."

"That's why I knew you had to tell Al," Sharon said. "It's my guess you'll tell them who you are, and I knew Al had to get used to the idea."

"What will your pa do when he hears about me?" Mark asked.

Burke spread his hands. "I dunno. He can be mighty mean and hardheaded, but damn it, if he draws on you, you'll have to kill him or be killed, and no man is gonna stand there and let himself be killed if he can help it."

"Suppose I kill him," Mark said, looking at Sharon. "What does that do to the way you feel about me?"

"I don't know," Sharon said slowly. "I have mixed-up feelings about pa. I hate him for many reasons, but he is my father, and I guess you can both love and hate a man. I think I would hate you if you went after him and killed him, but if he forces you into a fight, I could not blame you no matter how it turns out."

Mark rose. "I guess I'd better get out of here and start earning my pay, though I don't expect to see the Halls until they want us to."

"I'll be on the job at six in the morning," Burke said. "You'll have to stay awake all night. You can sleep tomorrow. I'll call you in time for the meeting. I want you to cruise the town every hour. It'll be a long night, but I think we've got to do it."

"Have you told the townspeople yet?"

Burke shook his head. "I've been thinking on it. I don't want to worry them before I have to. Besides, I don't see that they can help."

"Old men can pull triggers," Mark said.

"I know," Burke said. "It's just that it's our job."

"It's their town, too," Mark said.

Burke held up his hands in surrender. "You've convinced me. I'll tell 'em."

After Mark left, Sharon said, "What do you think pa will do when he hears about Mark?"

"He'll raise hell and prop it up with a stick," Burke said. "My God, we've got enough trouble. I didn't figure on anything like this."

"We can't let pa kill him," Sharon said. "I had a feeling about him the first time I saw him. I've known him only a little while, but I think I love him."

"Love him?" Burke demanded. "He only got to town on Monday."

Sharon smiled. "Oh, it's crazy, all right, but he's the only man I ever met I could marry."

Burke grinned. "There's not many around here and that's a fact. Well, sis, I've got a notion that he feels the same way about you."

"I think he does," she said. "Knowing pa, I expect the worst. We've got to save Mark."

"Pa will try to get him killed in one way or another," Burke said. "We can count on that." He looked at Sharon for a long moment, then he nodded. "All right, we'll try to keep Mark alive, but it won't be easy."

CHAPTER XVIII

For several days old man Hall had been expecting word from his Laramie connection as to when the money shipment from the East would be coming through on the train. When he hadn't heard by Friday morning, he was in a frenzy of rage. He cursed his wife. He struck his youngest son when he didn't move fast enough to suit the old man, and he finally wound up kicking his dog and sending him howling under the house.

By that time his middle son Larry had had enough. Larry was the only one of the three boys who had the temerity to challenge him, and that was exactly what he did. He said, "I don't know what the hell is riling you, but the dog didn't have anything to do with it."

"He was in my way," the old man snapped.

"You've been getting meaner by the minute," Larry said. "Now just what's wrong?"

"I ain't had word from Laramie," the old man said in the same snappish tone he had used before. "I gave Lange a thousand dollars to get word to us in time to get there. For all I know the damned train carrying the fifty thousand dollars has gone through and we've missed it."

"You don't know that," Larry said. "Maybe it was held up back in Omaha. You'll hear. Lange never has given you a bad tip. I don't figure he will this time."

"I tell you we were supposed to hear before this," the old man grumbled. "If I don't get word by tomorrow, I'm going up there and unscrew his head."

"No you won't," Larry said. "You've got too much to do here."

The old man wheeled and started to stalk away, then turned back. "You're right about that. I wonder how much dinero Jess keeps on the Bar B."

"Or how much Rodney has in his bank," Larry said.

The old man guffawed. "Well, we'll find out."

"If we don't hear in a couple more days," Larry said, "I say we hit Broken Bow and get to hell out of this country. We've been talking about getting square with the Burkes as long as I can remember, but it's just been talk. It's time we done something more'n talk."

"I know, I know," the old man said impatiently. "I just hate to miss a chance like that train was gonna give us. Your ma now, she's like you. She wants to go and says we've got enough dinero saved up. She claims she's got a bad feeling about the train job and she don't want us to do it, but damn it, we need more'n we've got now."

Larry looked the old man in the eyes. He said in a low tone, "Pa, I've got a notion you don't want to leave here ever. I think you're afraid to see what's going on outside. As far as you're concerned, your whole goddamn world is right here in this canyon."

If Larry had been either one of the other boys, the old man would have hit him, but he had a grudging respect for Larry, so he did no more than clench his fists. He glowered at Larry for a moment, then he said, "You go tell that squaw of your'n over yonder at Bullhide to get packed up. We'll be leaving in a day or two."

"She says she ain't going with me," Larry said glumly. "She's crazy about Al Burke."

"All bets are off with the sheriff when we hit Broken Bow," the old man said. "I figure he's gonna get his-self beefed before it's over. She can't marry a dead man, can she?"

"No, but . . ."

"Tell her," the old man shouted angrily. "If you want her, you can sure have her. We'll take her with us if we have to hog-tie her. We'll put her on the train with ma, and she can wait in Salt Lake City for us."

The old man wheeled again, and this time he strode across the yard to his front porch. He sat down, loaded his pipe and fired it, then leaned back in his rocker. A moment later he rose. A rider had come into view from the canyon below the house. Maybe it was the messenger he'd been waiting for. He stepped off the porch and walked down the slope toward the approaching rider.

A few minutes later the man reined up beside him. He asked, "You Victor Hall?"

"I am," the old man said.

The rider drew an envelope from his coat pocket and handed it to the old man, then turned his horse and rode back into the canyon without another word. The old man tore the envelope open and drew out the single sheet of paper. He unfolded it and read: "Wednesday. 10 P.M."

He laughed and wadded the paper up and tossed it to one side. He strode to the corral where his boys were breaking a new horse. He said, "We'll do the job Wednesday night. The train leaves Laramie at ten. We'll hit Broken Bow on Monday. That'll give us time to get ma and the squaw on the train."

"It's about time," Larry said. "I'm tired of waiting."

The other two nodded, and the old man walked back to the house and resumed his seat on the porch, the evil mood leaving him. Suddenly he felt fine. For the moment even his rheumatism didn't hurt him.

"Fetch me a cup of coffee," he yelled.

When his wife brought him the coffee, he felt good enough to fly. He said, "We're leaving here Tuesday. We'll put you and Larry's squaw on the train Wednesday afternoon. We'll see you in Salt Lake City sometime. I dunno just when."

"So you're bound to go ahead with the train job," his wife said. "You're a bullheaded, stupid old man, and don't start swearing at me again. If you do, I'll get on my horse and start for Laramie today, and you won't see me in Salt Lake City or anywhere else. You hear me?"

He glowered at her, thinking he had never seen her so angry. She didn't need to get her feathers ruffled like this, he thought resentfully, but he didn't say it. Usually she was very quiet and obedient, but there had been a few times when she had been pushed too far, and he had learned to respect her anger. This time she was furious because she had some kind of crazy hunch about the train robbery. Well, he wasn't going to be stopped by an old woman's fear, but he didn't say that, either.

"I hear real good." He turned his head to look down the canyon. Three riders had just come into view, and it took only one glance to identify them. "Them damned Dorn kids again," he muttered. "What do you suppose they want this time?"

He put his cup down and rose, his pipe clenched between his teeth. His good humor deserted him. He was angry because his privacy was being invaded again. He didn't like the Dorns anyway. He strode toward them, his anger growing with each step, but he never had a chance to say what he was thinking.

Before the Dorns reached him, the youngest one shouted, "I told you we didn't need you. We just proved it. We knocked over the Platte Junction bank by ourselves." He held up a partly filled sack. "Now we've got money. You think you're so high and mighty. I guess we showed you what we can do."

The old man stopped and stared at the Dorns who had reined up twenty feet from him. "You infernal idiots," he fumed. "Platte Junction is just across the line. You'll have a lawman on your tail in forty-eight hours. You take my word."

"Naw." Bud Dorn shook his head. "We had bandannas over our faces. They don't know who we are. I shot the banker. He won't be sending no lawman after us."

The old man was speechless with rage. All he could say was, "Why?"

"'Cause he came boiling out of his office wanting to know what was going on," Bud said. "It was easier to shoot him than to try telling him."

"We shot a kid when we were leaving town," one

135

of the other Dorns said. "It was a regular shooting gallery there for a while. Bud here got a slug in his leg."

The old man wished he'd got it between his eyes. He knew the banker in Platte Junction and he liked him. He had been a peaceful old man who wouldn't have used a gun under any circumstances. The Dorns weren't just infernal idiots. They were dangerous maniacs. There was no use talking to them.

"Get out of here," he said hoarsely.

"We're going into Broken Bow with you," one of them said. "When do we do it?"

The old man hesitated, wondering if they would be more trouble than they were worth. He had an idea how he could use them and get them killed to boot if he was lucky. He said, "Monday morning. Be here at sunup."

Bud held up the sack again and shook it. "Five hundred dollars we got," he said triumphantly. "I guess you won't be looking down your nose at us no more."

They whirled their horses and galloped down the canyon and disappeared from the old man's sight. Still he stood staring after them for a long time before he turned and trudged slowly back to his porch. The Dorns could not be trusted to do anything right. To rob a nearby bank and kill the banker and shoot a kid, all for a stinking five hundred dollars, was so stupid it was beyond belief.

One thing was sure. If they didn't follow his orders when they got to Broken Bow, he'd shoot them as quick as he would the sheriff or his deputy. He hoped they believed that when he told them.

CHAPTER XIX

Mark was awakened late Friday afternoon by a steady hammering on his door. He had been up all night cruising the town on the hour just as Al Burke had told him to do, and now it seemed that he was struggling slowly upward out of a bottomless pit. He put his feet on the floor and rubbed his face, hoping he was having a nightmare, but the pounding continued.

He rose, staggered to the door, and opened it. Al Burke stood there, grinning. "Well, son, you look as if you had been a long ways off and wasn't sure you wanted to come back."

"I have been and I'm not sure I do want to come back." Mark sat down on the bed again. "It was a long night, Al, and nothing happened."

Burke stepped into the room. "I figured it was that way, or I'd have heard from you. I'm sorry to make you miss your night's sleep, but we've got to do it until this business with the Halls goes one way or the other. I'll be going to Bullhide Monday afternoon. I'll find out then."

"Maybe you'd better not go," Mark said.

Burke shook his head. "I've got to. I guess you've heard the gossip that I go there to see Lucy Kline. I'm fixing to tell her that we're getting married Tuesday which is what she's been wanting. I've been afraid to marry her because I knew pa would split a gut over me marrying a half-breed."

Mark stared at him, shocked by the realization that this meant Al Burke and his father had parted company. He said, "So you really did it."

"That I have." Burke laughed sourly. "Ain't that a hell of a thing for a man to admit when he's almost thirty years old? I've wanted to do it as long as I can remember, but I've been afraid of pa."

"It is a hell of a thing to admit," Mark agreed, thinking it was a situation he could not understand because he'd had no father he could remember. "I still don't think you ought to go. I couldn't hold the Halls off by myself, and if I'm going to lose sleep for the next four or five days, I've got to believe there's a chance the Halls will do what you heard."

Burke walked to the window and stared into the street. "I guess I hadn't thought of it that way, but you're right. I can't ride out there during the day because that would mean you'd have to stay up all day, too." He shook his head. "No, Mark, I've got to go, but if the rumor has anything to it, I'll get right back to town. I don't want Lucy here anyhow if we're going to have the raid."

Mark rose and, going to the bureau, poured water into the basin. He asked, "You decided about telling the townspeople?"

"No, I ain't," Burke said. "It'll scare 'em to death, as old and half-sick as most of 'em are."

Mark looked at himself in the mirror and fingered his stubble. "I guess I ought to shave."

Burke shook his head. "Naw, leave it on. You look meaner this way."

Mark washed and dried his face, thinking that Burke was uneasy about this confrontation with his father even though they had broken. He poured the water into the slop jar, then ran a comb through his hair. He said, "If you don't tell 'em, and if the people are asleep as usual, and we have any kind of a wind, this town will go like it was made out of paper, and the people will burn to death in their beds."

Burke swore. "I know, but I guess I'd rather take that chance than to scare 'em before we know for sure about this deal." He rubbed his chin, then added slowly. "It's a hell of a decision to make. These people look to us for protection, and I ain't sure we're going to be able to give it to 'em. I guess I'll wait another day or two. Something is gonna happen that'll tell us how serious this is. I've got a hunch."

Mark buckled his gun belt around him, then put on his hat. "Let's get at it."

"You gonna tell pa and my uncles who you are?"

"I'll decide that after we start talking," Mark answered. "If your pa riles me, I will." He hesitated, then asked, "What will your pa do when he hears?"

"I've been thinking on that all day," Burke said. "He may pull his gun, but he hasn't tried to kill a man for a long time, so I don't figure he will. It's more likely he'll cuss you awhile, then threaten you, and if you're still here, wind up sending for a gunslick to kill you."

Mark stepped into the hall, Burke following. Mark

said, "If it comes to gunplay, stay out of it. I wouldn't expect any man to shoot his father."

"I hope to hell it don't come to that," Burke said, "but pa is like a volcano. Sometimes he just rumbles along making a lot of noise, but sometimes he erupts; and when he does, all hell busts loose."

They went down the stairs and across the lobby into the sun-drenched street. When they entered the bank, the teller jerked his thumb at the office and said, "They're waiting for you. Go on in."

"Like three judges before the execution," Burke said.

The teller grinned. "You might say that."

Burke led the way through the gate at the end of the counter. He said, "I always hate these meetings, mostly because what pa says becomes law and he's never open to any amendments."

When he knocked, a man bellowed, "Come in." Burke opened the door and stepped into the office. Mark, a step behind him, had his first look at Jess Burke. He was a big man with a jutting jaw and prominent chin. His eyes were blue, brittle and hard and piercing. His hair, gray at the temples, was brown.

It wasn't Jess Burke's features that struck Mark, although he had to admit to himself that knowing what the man had done had prejudiced him, but rather the feeling of ruthlessness, that Burke would ride over any man who stood in his way.

"Pa, this is my deputy, Mark Morgan," Al Burke was saying, "and Uncle Bob and Uncle Rodney."

The words jarred against Mark's ears and beat at them and were gone before he heard them, so intent had his attention been on Jess. Now he nodded, noting that the uncles were as unimpressive as he had expected.

Bob was skinny and withered far beyond what a man of his age should be, a sick man with a redness of face that might indicate a steady, low fever. Rodney was the opposite. He was fat, so fat that he seemed wedged into his swivel chair, so fat that even breathing was an effort.

Not one of the three men made any effort to shake hands. They looked Mark over as casually as they might have inspected a beef. After a time Jess asked, "What experience do you have, Morgan?"

"I was a deputy in Baca County before I came here," Mark answered.

"Why did you quit there and come here asking for a job?" Jess demanded, his tone brusque and insulting. "Were you fired?"

Anger began building in Mark. He had hoped to get through this interview without losing his temper, but suddenly he was afraid he wasn't going to be able to control himself. Here he was at last, facing the men who had murdered his father and uncle, men who had robbed him of what had been a good ranch, men who had deprived him of a normal home. He clenched his fists, his right one close to the butt of his gun.

"No, if it's any of your business," he said, his tone as brusque and insulting as Jess Burke's. "I was not fired. I came here partly because I wanted the salary Converse County is offering a deputy. I see no reason to meet here with you and your brothers asking for your approval. I was hired by the sheriff. I'll answer to him."

141

Jess Burke's face turned red. He started to get up, then dropped back. He said, "Maybe you don't understand the situation in Converse County. We . . ."

"I understand it, all right," Mark said. "I don't like any part of you or your brothers butting into the sheriff's business. I was told by Al that you refused to permit any of your men to help protect the town from the Halls, so let us alone and we'll do the job for you by ourselves."

This time Jess was on his feet, trembling in anger. He shouted, "Al, fire this bastard. He's got too big a mouth for the job."

His brothers nodded agreement. Al had been grinning as if he enjoyed hearing Mark talk to his father as he had always wanted to but had never been tough enough to do. Then Mark wondered if the grin was hiding Al's uneasiness, and he began to wonder if Al would back him up.

He had the answer to the question immediately. Al said coldly, "I reckon not, pa. I need him."

"I said fire him, damn it," Jess roared, jabbing a forefinger in Mark's direction. "And you get out of the county, mister. I don't want no smart-ass gabber like you in Converse County."

"I'll stay here long enough to take care of the Halls," Mark said. "There's something else you'd better know, Burke. It explains the real reason I'm here. My right name ain't Morgan. I was raised by Kate Morgan, so I took her name. My real name is Cardigan. Flint Cardigan was my father."

Jess sat down again, suddenly, as if his knees could no longer support him. His mouth sprung open, and spit dribbled down his chin before he realized it was there and wiped it off with his sleeve. His brothers were paralyzed, Bob looking as if he were going to faint. All three were dumbfounded, shocked into silence and immobility.

For a long moment there was no sound in the room except the buzzing of a fly against a window and the steady ticking of the clock on the wall above Rodney's head. Then Jess asked hoarsely, "Can you prove it?"

"I wouldn't even try," Mark said scornfully. "I don't have to prove anything to you or anyone else. I'm not like these poor devils in Converse County who are under your thumb. I'm only sorry I wasn't old enough to help my father fight when you murdered him and my uncle."

"I suppose you came back to kill us," Jess said. "Well, we'll see about that. I'll have you hanging from a tree limb before the week's out."

"There ain't much of the week left," Mark said. "And if you hang me, you'll get wiped out by the Halls along with your brothers. Al can't fight ten men himself."

Slowly Jess turned his gaze to Al. "You knew who he is all the time?"

"Yeah, I knew," Al said. "I needed a deputy. He's a good man. I have a letter from Sheriff Abe Gilroy of Baca County." He waggled a finger at his father. "I don't want no more lynch talk, pa. If you try hanging him or sending for some gunslick to smoke him down, I'll arrest you as soon as I would any other man."

Jess Burke was sick. He wiped his face with his bandanna, and sweat immediately popped through the pores of his skin again. For a moment Mark thought he was going to throw up on the bank office floor. He moistened his lips with the tip of his tongue.

"What's got into you, boy?" he asked. "This ain't like you."

"You told me I was old enough to wipe my own nose," Al said. "That's what I'm doing. Mark is my deputy, and he'll be my deputy as long as I'm sheriff if he wants the job." He turned to the door. "Let's slope out of here, Mark."

"You, Morgan or Cardigan or whatever your name is," Jess shouted. "You listen to me. You think you're scaring us, don't you? You think we'll deed over Cardigan valley to you just because you claim to be the son of a man who died here twenty years ago. Well, it won't work."

"Don't say my father died, damn it," Mark said in a low tone. "He was murdered. If you want to kill me, go ahead and make your try. I like to see the face of the man who's trying to shoot me."

"Get out," Jess said, motioning to the door. "Get out of here."

"In answer to your question about expecting you to deed Cardigan valley over to me," Mark said, "no, I don't expect that. It's hard to imagine a man who murdered my father and uncle and would have murdered me and my aunt if you'd caught us to ever do a decent thing. You'll never change, Burke. I'm not stupid enough to believe that you will."

He turned quickly and stalked out of the office and across the bank and on into the late afternoon sunlight. Al Burke caught up with him, and they walked slowly toward Sharon's Beanery.

"You sore at me for what I said to your pa?" Mark asked.

"Hell no," Al said, a tight grin curling his lips. "He had it coming. I guess no man ever talked that way to him in his life. Not and lived anyway. He'll never get over it." Then he shook his head. "But watch your back. You've got both the Dorns and pa gunning for you. Well, let's go tell Sharon how it went."

CHAPTER XX

Late Saturday afternoon a man walked into the sheriff's office, looked at Al Burke, then at Mark, and said, "I want to talk to the sheriff." He was a tall, weather-beaten man with cowboy written all over him. The fact that he was wearing a star startled Burke because few lawmen had visited Converse County since he had been sheriff.

Burke rose and extended his hand. "I'm the sheriff, Al Burke. What can I do for you?"

"I'm Luke Darby," the man said, shaking Burke's hand. "Deputy from Albany County, Wyoming. I hope you can do quite a bit for me. We had a bank robbery in Platte Junction a few days ago. One man was killed, a banker named Jason Foster. A boy in the street was shot as the outlaws were leaving town, too, but I guess he'll live. We think they might be from your county."

Burke nodded at Mark who was sitting on the other side of the office. He said, "Darby, meet my deputy, Mark Morgan." The two men shook hands, then Burke said, "The Halls live in Converse County. We've had rumors about them holding up banks and trains for years, but we never had any proof, and you're the first Wyoming law man to come asking about them."

"I've heard of the Halls," Darby said, "but I don't figure the Halls done this one. Grabbing them and holding them is like keeping a cloud of smoke in your hands. They're professionals and smart as hell. We don't really know much about 'em because they don't make mistakes, but these bastards were amateurs. Kids, we think. They were wearing bandannas, so we can't identify them except by voice. They took what the teller had in his cage, but never touched the safe. They got maybe five hundred dollars when they could have had five thousand."

Burke thought about the Dorn boys, but for all of their meanness he had never heard any rumors about them being involved in bank robberies. It didn't seem to be their kind of antic. He said, "I guess we've got a few candidates. You got anything else to go on?"

Darby nodded. "There were three of 'em. One stayed outside and held the horses. Two came into the bank and threw their guns on the teller and told him to put all of his money into a sack that they shoved at him.

"They talked all the time they were doing it, one in particular who kept running off at the mouth about how the Halls wouldn't be so damned big now. That was what made us think they came from here. Jason Foster heard them and came out of his office to see what was going on, and the one who gabbed so much shot him for no reason.

"They told the teller to lie on the floor and they cleared out, but some of the businessmen heard the shot and ordered them to stop. They started shooting wild at anything they saw. That was when the boy got hit. The townsmen shot back and think they wounded one of 'em."

"That still don't prove much." Burke shook his head. "The Halls have been talked about and written about until they're close to being legends. I'm not sure why so much has been said about 'em except that they live by themselves out there on the North Fork. I guess the main thing is that while they're gone, somebody pulls a big job."

"That's right," Darby said. "Maybe their talking about the Halls don't prove anything, but we thought it was worth riding down here for. We don't even know these bandits were kids except they weren't big men and they got worked up like they'd been drinkin'. The gabby one who talked so much had a high-pitched voice, but it might have been because he was excited. I suppose that was why he shot Foster. He was just trigger crazy." Darby paused, then added, "There was one more thing. They stunk. The teller said he had never smelled anything like it. Reminded him of buffalo hunters in the old days."

Burke slapped a hand to his forehead. "By God, Mark did you hear that?"

"I guess it's all the identification you need," Mark said.

"You know who they were?" Darby asked.

"We know," Burke said. "The Dorn boys. They've been in trouble, and we suspect them of killing the three deputies I had before Morgan here hired on, but this is the first robbery I've heard of where they might be suspects. They live on the North Fork close to the Halls, so I guess it'd be natural to want to impress 'em."

"When can we take them?" Darby asked.

"In the morning," Burke answered. "It's too far to start tonight." He scratched his head. "It may be a chore, though. They're the crazy kind who'll shoot first before they've got any reason to shoot."

He glanced thoughtfully at Mark, tapping his fingers on the top of his desk. "I was figuring on taking you, but I guess I can't risk leaving town without a lawman." He brought his gaze back to Darby. "We'll leave as soon as we can get breakfast. The only restaurant we have opens at six."

"I'll be waiting for the door to open," Darby said and left the office.

Burke leaned back in his chair, a sour expression on his face. "Ain't that the damnedest thing? As if we didn't have enough trouble with the Halls."

"I was thinking while Darby was talking that there might be a connection," Mark said.

Burke shook his head. "I don't see it."

"Well, you said they live close together, and you likewise said you'd heard in Bullhide that the Halls were planning on one more big job before they left the country. Maybe the Dorns are figuring on going, too. They know they're in trouble here in town after I jailed 'em the other night. Now it just might be they want to go with the Halls."

"And the old man Hall don't want 'em, but they figure they can prove they can rob a bank as well as he can." Burke rubbed the back of his neck. "Yeah, it makes a little sense. From all I hear about the old man, he's smart and practical, and he's sure never made the kind of mistake that gets him arrested, so he wouldn't want the Dorns, as crazy as they are. Well,

I hope we don't have to take the Halls on, too, when we arrest the Dorns."

Burke rose. "Well, it's six o'clock, so it's up to you. I guess you'd better sleep tomorrow. If anything goes wrong, you'll hear about it in a hurry. Damn it, I wish we knew what the Halls were thinking."

"Maybe you'll pick up something tomorrow in Bull-hide," Mark said.

Burke nodded, thinking of Lucy. "I'll stop there and see if Pat Kline has heard anything. The Halls do their drinking in his place, and sometimes it loosens their tongues."

He left the courthouse and walked slowly to his place, his thoughts lingering on Lucy. He was glad in one way that Darby had showed up. At least he had an excuse to see her and tell her they would soon be married.

CHAPTER XXI

Al Burke and Luke Darby left Broken Bow early Sunday morning, the air cold and damp. Storm clouds were building up above the continental divide to the west, with lightning slashing downward toward the peaks. The rumble of thunder came to them across the rolling land of the park. Burke expected the storm to hit them before they reached the North Fork, but instead it shifted to slam across the southern half of the park. By the time they reached the Bullhide Inn, the sky had cleared.

Darby shook his head as they dismounted and tied in front of the inn. "A hell of a place to live," he said, looking up at the steep canyon wall.

"This used to be a booming mining camp," Burke said. "Pat Kline who runs the inn was here then. He can tell some good stories."

"You say the Halls and Dorns have always lived here?" Darby asked.

"The Dorns have," Burke answered. "The Halls have been here for twenty years." He thought about saying that was when his father had driven them out of the park but decided it wasn't the thing to say.

He jerked his head toward the inn. "Come on in. I want to talk to Pat. I'll buy you a drink."

"That's an offer I never refuse," Darby said, grinning.

Kline was surprised when he saw Burke. "Ain't you a day early?"

"We've got business with the Dorns." Burke introduced Darby, then said, "He's from Albany County. The Dorn boys held up the bank in Platte Junction and killed a man."

"Yeah, they were in here bragging about it," Kline said in disgust. "I knew Jason Foster. A hell of a fine old man. I told them bastards what I thought of 'em, but they just laughed in my face." He shook his head. "But I dunno about you two taking 'em in. If all three are home, you'll never root 'em out. It'd take a posse to do the job."

"I dunno where I'd get a posse in this county," Burke said sourly. "What do you hear about the Halls?"

"Nothing more than I told you the last time you were here," Kline said. "They aim to hit Broken Bow, all right. It'll be purty quick. Maybe tomorrow."

Burke motioned to Darby. "Give him a drink, Pat. Where's Lucy?"

"In her room as far as I know," Kline said, reaching for a bottle.

"I'll be right back," Burke told Darby and took the stairs two at a time.

He knocked on Lucy's door. She called, "Come in." He opened the door and stepped inside. She was sitting by the window, sewing. She laid the partly made dress on the bed and rose, holding out her

152

arms to Burke. "I saw you and another man ride in. You're a day early."

He walked toward her, grinning. "A surprise, honey," he said and took her into his arms.

When she drew her lips from his, she whispered, "Have we got time?"

"I'm sorry," he said. "I wish we did, but I've got a job to do. The reason I came up to see you is to tell you we're going to get married as soon as you come to town. I don't want you there if the Halls raid Broken Bow. You'll be safer here, but as soon as that's over . . ."

"Al, I'm not safe here," she interrupted. "Larry Hall has been after me to go with him when they leave. He's been talking about Tuesday."

"That means they'll hit us on Monday," Burke said, "or early Tuesday morning."

"He says I'm going with him whether I like it or not," she said. "He says they'll hog-tie me and put me on a horse and take me. I'm scared, Al."

Burke turned from her to the window and stared through it as blankly as if his eyes were shut. It seemed to him that the walls were closing in on him, that there was no way he could meet all the problems that were threatening him.

"My God, Lucy," he said in a troubled tone, "why would he make you do something you didn't want to do?"

"He says they're going to kill you," she said. "He says I can't marry a dead man."

He wheeled to face her. "I can't take you with me now. I'm going after the Dorns, and I figure that'll be a tough job. Maybe you'd better not leave here when it's daylight. Chances are they've got a man watching the inn, but if you think it'd be safer in town, then you'd better make a run for it after dark. If you can't find me, go to Sharon's Beanery. Sharon's my sister."

He kissed her again and, wheeling, strode out of the room without looking back. If he was killed today —and he knew the chances were good that he would be—he wondered what would happen to Lucy. Maybe she would go with Larry Hall rather than stay here in Bullhide. He couldn't expect Sharon to look out for her and her baby.

"Let's ride," he said to Darby and walked on past him through the door.

"You know where the Dorns live?" Darby asked as he caught up with Burke.

"It ain't far from here." Burke nodded at an opening in the canyon wall. "The Halls live up that canyon about a mile from the creek. The Dorns are in the next side canyon. It's another quarter of a mile."

Darby kept staring at the side of the canyon above him. "There's enough trees and boulders up yonder to hide a dozen men. I've got a feeling in my gut we're being watched."

"I get that feeling every time I come here," Burke said. "I figure it's the Halls, but they've never bothered me. I don't think the Dorns are smart enough to put a guard out. They never think past the day they're living."

"I hope you're right," Darby said worriedly.

They rode downstream. A few minutes later Burke said, "We'll leave our horses here. We'll go the rest of the way on foot. If we rode up to their front door, they'd blow us out of our saddles before we ever got there."

They dismounted and left their horses in the willows on the bank of the North Fork, then started up the narrow trail that led up through the side canyon. A few minutes later Burke motioned for Darby to stop. He nodded at the dilapidated shack that clung precariously to a ledge on their right. A small stream trickled down the bottom canyon, a few low willows dotting the banks. A pole corral was on the opposite side of the stream, its only occupant a skinny bay gelding.

"There ain't much cover between here and the shack," Darby grumbled.

"No," Burke agreed, "but we'll use what there is, and maybe we'll get lucky. If they were all here, we'd see three horses in the corral, so maybe the one who was wounded is the only one who's home."

"Sounds reasonable," Darby agreed. "I'll settle for one."

"We'll take him in and use him for bait," Burke said.

"What do you mean by that?"

"We'll lock him up, and the other two will try to break him out of jail," Burke answered. "They're like a pack of wolves. Being penned up makes 'em crazier'n they are normally. The other two know that, so they'll make a try at getting him out."

Darby sucked in a long breath. "I don't like the setup. If he spots us, it'd be like shooting fish in a barrel."

"If we don't make any noise and if we crowd the cliff, I don't think he'll see us till we're there," Burke said. "Then we'll make a run from the wall of the canyon to the door."

He started up the steep slope, leaving the trail to

hug the canyon wall and moving carefully and slowly so he wouldn't kick any rocks loose. Darby followed. About halfway to the shack Darby kicked a rock that plummeted down the slope and started a small avalanche, the rumble sounding inordinately loud to Burke.

They froze, watching the single window beside the door of the shack, but there was no movement. They went on, Burke still leading, not stopping until they were opposite the corner of the shack and about ten feet from it. They paused there a moment listening, then he nodded at Darby and plunged to the door in three long strides. He slammed it open and went in fast, his gun in his hand.

The youngest Dorn boy was the only one in the shack. He lay in a bunk. But the instant the door opened, he sat up and reached for his gun that was on the table a few feet from him.

"Don't try it, Bud," Burke said. "You're under arrest for the robbery of the Platte Junction bank and the murder of Jason Foster."

The stench inside the shack made it impossible to take a full breath. Filth was everywhere. Dirty dishes were stacked on the table. A greasy frying pan was on the stove. The dirt floor had not been swept for weeks.

Darby had come inside, but he began backing out immediately, muttering, "I'll go saddle his horse."

Dorn put his feet on the floor. "I've got a bad leg," he said. "I can't walk."

One pants leg had been rolled to his knee. A dirty, bloody cloth was wrapped around the calf of his leg. Burke asked, "Where are your brothers?"

"Hunting," Dorn grunted. "Don't do you no good to take me to town. They'll get me out of the jug."

"I hope they try," Burke said.

He took a notebook from his coat pocket and tore out a sheet. Finding a stubby pencil in his pocket, he wrote: "I am arresting Bud for the murder of Jason Foster and the robbery of the Platte Junction bank. Both of you are wanted for murder and bank robbery. Come in and give yourselves up. You'll save trouble and some lives."

He knew they would laugh at his order, but at least it told them where Bud was, and it would bring them to town. He left the note on the table, handed Bud his hat, and pulled him to his feet.

"Damn it, I told you I couldn't walk," Dorn yelled.

"Put your right arm around my shoulders," Burke said. "Keep the foot of your wounded leg off the floor, and put your weight on me when you take a step."

By the time they reached the door, Darby had brought the saddled horse from the corral. They lifted Dorn aboard, then started down the trail to the North Fork, Darby leading the horse. Burke glanced at the boy's flushed face, wondering how badly the wound was infected. His usual brashness had gone out of him. He'd be lucky if he didn't lose his leg, Burke thought.

They reached their horses, mounted, and started up the North Fork. They glanced back often, then lifted their eyes to the canyon wall, wondering if they were being watched, but if any of the Halls were hidden on that rocky slope, they gave no indication of it. What Burke feared most was the possibility that the other two Dorn boys might get back from their hunt and start in pursuit, but it didn't happen.

It wasn't until they topped the west ridge that they felt they were in the clear. Darby said softly, "I never cotton to the notion of being ambushed. I sure figured it would happen before we got out of that hole."

"We were lucky," Burke said.

He glanced at Bud swaying in the saddle, his teeth clenched against the pain that must be constant and agonizing. He said, "We'll call Doc Jones as soon as we get to town, so hang on, boy."

Dorn was clutching the saddle horn with both hands. Apparently he hadn't heard what Burke said. They'd do well, he thought, if they got the boy to town.

CHAPTER XXII

Mark was in the sheriff's office late Sunday afternoon when Al Burke and Luke Darby brought Bud Dorn in. They were almost carrying him, and Burke, jerking his head at Mark, said, "Fetch Doc Jones. This kid's in bad shape." When Mark started toward the door, Burke added, "He's over the bank."

"I know," Mark said. "I've seen his sign."

He had no reason to love any of the Dorn tribe, Mark thought wryly as he strode rapidly to the doctor's office. Any one of them would have killed him if the opportunity had come, but here he was, going for the doctor for the worst of the Dorns.

Mark had not met Doc Jones before. He was surprised that the doctor was younger than most of the men he had seen in Broken Bow, probably not over fifty. He was a tall, awkward-appearing man with an Ichabod Crane kind of loping walk. The instant that Mark said the sheriff wanted him, he picked up his bag and started toward the door.

"He's at the jail?" Jones asked as he went down the stairs.

Mark, three steps above him, said, "That's right."

He stood with Darby and Burke and watched as Jones unwrapped the dirty cloth from Dorn's leg. The doctor shook his head, asking, "Why didn't you come to me in the first place? If you'd waited another twenty-four hours, you'd have lost that leg."

"I didn't come to you this time," Dorn muttered. "They brung me."

"He shot the banker in Platte Junction," Burke said. "That's why he didn't want to come to you."

When Jones finished cleaning and wrapping the wound, he rose and snapped his bag shut. "Stay off that leg, boy," he said.

Burke laughed. "He ain't going anywhere, Doc."

"I figger I am," Dorn said. "I won't be here this time tomorrow. You'll see."

Outside in the sheriff's office Jones said, "I don't like the looks of that leg, Sheriff. I may have to cut it off, and I'm not sure he'll live through the operation. He's a damned sick boy."

"Don't make no difference, does it, Doc?" Darby asked. "If he don't die here, he'll hang in Wyoming."

Jones stared at him for a moment as if debating with himself about arguing with Darby, then he shook his head and walked past him in his strange, awkward stride, calling back, "I'll drop by in the morning, Sheriff."

After he had left the courthouse, Burke said, "He didn't like your question, Darby. It hurt his professional pride."

"Well, it'll hurt mine if that bastard don't hang," Darby said.

"Let's go put the feed bag on," Burke said. "You'd better sleep here tonight. Mark will be in and out, and I'll be here in a couple of minutes if I hear any shooting. I don't figure they'll come tonight, but bringing the boy in may change their schedule."

After they left, Mark sat on the front steps of the courthouse smoking a cigarette. He told himself that it wasn't any more peculiar for him to have gone after the doctor for young Dorn than it was for him to be serving as deputy in Converse County at a time like this, defending Broken Bow and saving the Burkes' property.

At one time the Burkes would have killed him as certainly as the Dorns would today. As soon as this trouble was over, he'd head back to Baca County and a job with Sheriff Gilroy. He'd rid himself of his nightmares, and that was what he had come for. Then he thought of Sharon, and he wasn't so sure.

When Darby and Burke returned from having supper, Burke said, "Lucy Kline may show up tonight. If she does, she'll probably come to the jail. She don't know where I live, so you fetch her to my place."

Mark nodded, wondering why Lucy was coming to Broken Bow in the middle of the night; but Burke gave no explanation, so Mark didn't ask. He had his supper, made his first round of the town, and returned to the courthouse. For a time he sat talking with Darby who told him how they had taken young Dorn. Presently Darby went to bed, and Mark stepped outside.

It was a long night, longer than the previous night because there was a good chance that the other two Dorns might come in to release Bud whether the Halls made their raid tonight or not. He was tense as he moved around town listening for unusual sounds, his eyes continually probing the darkness for movement.

He had no idea how the raiders would come, or when, so all he could do was to stay awake and listen.

Near dawn he heard a horse coming in from the north. He rose from the courthouse steps where he had been sitting and drew his gun as he backed up against the front wall of the building. The sky was clear, the stars were out, and there was a thin wafer of a moon overhead, but the light was still too thin for him to see who it was.

The horse stopped in front of the courthouse. Silence for a moment, then he heard what he took for low sobbing. He wasn't sure, but when he saw a dim figure coming from the street toward him, he decided it must be Lucy Kline.

He waited until the newcomer had almost reached the courthouse steps before he asked, "Lucy?"

She whirled and started to run, but he caught her before she had gone far. "I'm the deputy, Morgan," he said. "I'll take you to Al."

She had started to fight him, but she stopped when she heard who he was. She clung to him, her sobs louder now. He patted her back and told her she was safe, that they'd find Al Burke.

It took little more than a minute to circle the courthouse and reach Burke's house, but she kept on crying softly. She was hysterical, Mark thought, and couldn't stop. Burke came out of the house immediately, and Lucy fell into his arms, crying louder than ever. Burke led her inside and lighted a lamp, then sat down and pulled her down on his lap.

"You're all right, honey," he said. "You'll be all right now."

It was several minutes before she became quiet. When she did, he asked, "What happened?"

Again several minutes passed before she could talk. When she did, the words came slowly. She said, "The Halls came in early this evening and started to drink. They got to arguing with pa about me going with them when they left. Pa said I wasn't going if I didn't want to, but the old man got mad and said I was going anyhow, that Larry could have me if he wanted me.

"I stood outside my room and listened to them. They kept saying there wouldn't be anything left of Broken Bow when they got done with it. They knew you had arrested Bud Dorn, and they said they were going to break him out of jail and then burn the town. As soon as it was dark, I slipped down the stairs and went out through the back door."

She stopped and clung to Burke as if afraid this wasn't real, as if she were afraid this was a pleasant dream following a terrifying nightmare.

"They won't get you, Lucy," Burke said. "You're safe."

"I was awful scared," she said finally. "I was more scared than I'd ever been before in my life. I think they would have killed me and pa, too, if they'd heard me leaving. Maybe they will kill pa if they find out what I did."

She started to sniffle again. Burke, a little impatient now, said, "You're all right, Lucy. I won't let them have you. You can trust me."

"I saddled my horse," she said, still speaking very slowly, "and led him around the buildings in a big circle. Every second I thought they'd hear me and come rushing out after me. I got across the creek and started up the trail. It seemed like my horse was making more noise than he ever had, snorting and grunting and kicking rocks loose. It was so dark, Al. I couldn't even see the trail most of the time when we were in the timber. I just didn't think I'd ever get here."

"Did you hear them say when they planned to make the raid?" Mark asked.

"They're leaving the North Fork early this morning," she said. "Old man Hall was awful mad because he couldn't get as many men as he had thought he could. He'll just have his boys and the Dorns."

"That'll be plenty," Burke said. "They'll get here before noon." He thought about it a moment, then he pushed Lucy off his lap. "I'm taking you to Sharon's place. You stay inside when they get here so they won't see you. They won't know where to look for you. Mark, put her horse away, then you go to bed."

Mark left the house, thinking that he wouldn't do much sleeping. They had been expecting the raid for so long, and the time was nearly here. As he walked back to the courthouse to get Lucy's horse, it struck him that a smart outlaw like old man Hall wouldn't risk his life getting a crazy, wounded kid like Bud Dorn out of jail. There was just one thing in Broken Bow he'd really be interested in . . . the bank.

CHAPTER XXIII

The Hall party left the North Fork in the gray, cold light of dawn, the old man in the lead, Larry behind him, his other sons behind Larry, and the two Dorn boys in the rear. There was no talk once they were under way. Before they started, the Dorns announced they were not going unless the Halls intended to help break Bud out of jail. The old man agreed, then he said, "But you'd better be damned sure you're willing to obey my order. I don't want you or nobody else bollixing things up at the last."

The Dorns nodded, but when the old man swung off the road into Broken Bow and headed across the park toward the Bar B, the Dorns galloped up to ride beside the old man, the oldest demanding, "Where in the hell do you think you're going? The jail's in Broken Bow and Broken Bow was straight ahead."

The old man kept the same steady pace he had been riding. He said, "You gonna start augerin' now after what we agreed on?"

"We've got a right to know . . ."

"You've got no right if you're riding with me," the old man snapped. "If you want to do the job yourself, go right ahead. Otherwise get back to where you were."

The Dorns looked at each other, then reined up and fell in behind the Halls. The old man grinned and winked at Larry who had come up to ride beside him. He said, "Them squirts ain't so tough."

"All they're thinking about is Bud," Larry said.

"Bud ain't who I'm thinking about," the old man said. "All I'm thinking about is Jess Burke."

"You aiming to take on the whole Bar B crew?" Larry demanded.

"I don't figger the Bar B crew is gonna be around here at this time of day," the old man answered. "They'll be scattered all over the park."

Fifteen minutes later they reined up in front of the Bar B house. For a time the old man sat his saddle, his gaze moving from the house to the big barn, to the corrals that held several horses, and on to the various outbuildings. The place was clean and neat and well laid out, the spread of a wealthy and meticulous man.

"He's got it good," the old man said softly. "Real good. How much blood like the Cardigan blood went into building this layout, and how much of other people's money like the Hall money went into it?"

No one answered. He had expected no answer. He stepped down and tied, then glanced around again. The only signs of life were plumes of smoke rising from the chimneys of the cookshack and the main house.

"Real quiet just like I figgered," the old man said. "I want you Dorns to take a look around the corrals

166

and the barn. If you find anybody, bring 'em to me. Duke and Rafe," he motioned to his youngest and oldest sons, "you go into the cookshack and tie the cook up so he won't make us no trouble. Larry, you come along with me."

He strode up the walk to the front door. The others were on the ground now, their mounts tied. The Dorn boys hesitated, still disgruntled about making this side trip. Larry said, "You kids had better do what pa says. If you start dragging your heels, he might take a notion to smoke you down and be done with you. If that happens, Bud never will get out of the jug."

They exchanged sullen glances, then started toward the barn. Larry caught up with his father who didn't hesitate when he reached the front door. He simply opened it and went in as if he owned the place; then he stopped and looked around the big, comfortably furnished room, a tight smile on his face.

"Yes, old Jess has had it real good," he murmured, "while me and your ma and you boys were stuck out there in that goddamned canyon."

He heard someone in the kitchen and crossed the living room to the kitchen door. He called, "Where's Jess?"

The housekeeper came out of the pantry and stood staring at him as if she couldn't believe any stranger would walk in the way he had. She asked, "Who are you?"

"Let's say I'm a neighbor who came to pay my respects to the great Jess Burke," the old man said. "Now where is he?"

"I don't know," the woman said. "I haven't seen

him since breakfast. Usually he goes into his office, but he might have gone out to the barn or corrals."

"Where's his office?"

"It's the door on the right as you came in," she said. "I'll go see if he's . . ."

"I'll go," the old man said. "You get to your cooking. There'll be six of us for dinner."

He wheeled past Larry and crossed the living room. He opened the door and stepped into the office. Jess was sitting at his desk studying a legal-looking document. He looked up when he heard the door open, then froze. The old man had not seen him for years, but he told himself Jess hadn't changed much. He just looked a little more prosperous than he used to.

"How are you, Jess?" the old man said softly.

Jess rose, moistened his lips with the tip of his tongue, then went for his gun. The old man shot him in the chest before his Colt was clear of leather, and shot him again through the belly as he started to fall. He moved forward, saw that Jess was dead, then turned to the open safe behind the desk.

Larry stood staring at him, openmouthed. "You ain't slowed up much, pa."

"I don't figger on slowing up until I settle down on the other side of the Rio Grande," the old man said.

He began pawing through the safe. The housekeeper ran into the room, saw Jess's body, and began backing away, her hand raised to her throat. The old man looked around, saw her, and rose. He said, "You get back to your cooking. I told you we was staying for dinner. Six of us."

"I won't cook for no murderers like you," the woman

said hoarsely. "You get out of here and take your gang with you."

The old man started pacing toward her, his right hand dropping to the butt of his gun. "I've never killed a woman in my life, but maybe it's time I was starting. Now I ain't of a mind to auger with you about it."

"Better do what he says, ma'am," Larry said.

The woman whirled and ran back into the kitchen. The old man turned to the safe again and started to pull papers from their pigeonholes and to litter the floor with them. Then he found what he was looking for, a buckskin bag that was half-full of something heavy. He opened it and looked inside, then lifted his gaze to meet Larry's.

"Mostly gold," he said, grinning, "and a few greenbacks. I figured Jess would have a chunk of dinero hid away."

He crossed the room to Larry. "Now after dinner we'll mosey into town. You and Duke and the Dorns will go to work on the courthouse. Tell the Dorns to go in shooting. You and Duke will be at the window of the sheriff's office. You'll take Al Burke and his deputy from there, only don't shoot 'em until the Dorns are dead. It'll save us the trouble of killing 'em. We can't afford to have 'em pestering us. Just be sure of one thing. Get Al Burke."

"I don't like it," Larry said. "It's a mighty goddamned cold-blooded business."

The old man snorted. "Of course it is. You think it wasn't cold blooded when the Burkes murdered the Cardigans. Or when Jess put a gun to my head and made me sell him my land? What do you think I've been dreaming about all these years? Now I'm gonna make my dream come true. We're gonna wipe the Burkes out except for the girl, and I figger it wouldn't be right to kill her.

"While you and Duke are taking care of the courthouse, me'n Rafe will call on Rodney Burke in the bank and withdraw all of his money, and then we'll kill him. If nothing happens to make us leave town in a hurry, we'll step into the store and rub Bob out. I hear he ain't gonna live long anyhow, so it don't make much difference about him. Maybe we'd do him a favor to shoot him, and I don't hanker to do the Burkes no favors."

The old man walked into the front room and sat down in a rocking chair, dropping the buckskin bag on the floor beside him. He filled his pipe and fired it, then said, "Go out and harness up a team. Jess must have a wagon around somewhere. Hook up and bring it to the front of the house. We'll put Jess in it. As soon as we finish eating, we'll send the woman and the cook into town with word that we'll be along to take Bud Dorn out of jail."

"You're going to warn them?" Larry demanded. "That's loco, pa."

"Oh no, it ain't." The old man laughed. "No sirree bob. It's smart. I tell you I've dreamed about this and planned it for a long time, though I didn't know Bud Dorn was gonna get himself jailed. That's another little fact that's in our favor. You see, they'll be watching the courthouse, and they won't expect us to tackle the bank till we've got Bud out of jail." He motioned toward the door. "Go on. Do what I've been telling you."

"What about Lucy?"

"We'll find her," the old man answered. "Broken

Bow ain't such a big town that she can hide. Chances are she'll be at Al Burke's place or his sister's restaurant."

Larry left the house, scowling and shaking his head. The old man continued to rock as he pulled on his pipe, his gaze once more moving around the big room. He nodded and said aloud, "Yes sir, Jess, you've had it good. But all it got you in the end was a quick trip to hell. I'm just sorry I waited so damned long to start you on that trip."

CHAPTER XXIV

Mark slept late on Monday morning. When he went into Sharon's Beanery for breakfast, he found Sharon behind the counter, yawning and sleepy eyed, but she managed a cheery, "Good morning," to Mark.

He took a seat on one of the stools and ordered flapjacks and bacon, then asked, "How's Lucy?"

"She's all right," Sharon answered. "Just scared, and I guess she's got a right to be. She's sure that the Halls will hunt till they find her, and when they do, they'll take her with them."

"We won't let them do it," Mark said. "Tell her that."

"It wouldn't do any good," Sharon said. "Al kept telling her that last night, but she can't believe that you two and this Wyoming deputy can hold them off. What she's really afraid of is that Al will get killed." She shrugged. "Well, I guess we can't do anything. We've just got to wait till it's over."

"Do you have a gun here?"

Sharon nodded. "A shotgun."

"If the Halls get the best of us, keep the scattergun

handy. It's a mighty persuasive weapon. Now, how about my flapjacks?"

"Coming right up," Sharon said and ran into the kitchen.

After he had finished eating, he slid off the stool and dropped a coin on the counter. He said, "I'd better find Al and hear what he's fixing to do."

"He's been in to see Lucy," Sharon said. "He's probably back in his office by now." She hesitated, then said, "Mark, I feel sorry for Lucy. This is all so strange to her. She's spent her life out there on the North Fork, and to her Broken Bow is a big city. We stayed up the rest of the night and talked. She seems like a fine girl. I didn't think a breed girl could be so pretty, and so . . . so sensible."

"She'll get used to this big city," Mark said and left the restaurant.

As soon as he stepped into the street, he heard the pound of hoofs and the clatter of a wagon. He saw it immediately coming in from the north, the horses on a dead run, the driver applying his whip as hard as he could.

Mark's anger began to boil. There was no sense in running horses that hard, and he stepped off the boardwalk with the intention of hauling the driver down off his seat and giving him a lesson on the proper handling of horses. A thoroughly frightened woman sat beside the driver, hanging on with both hands.

The instant the driver stopped the wagon in front of the hotel, he bawled, "Jess Burke has been murdered."

Mark forgot all about teaching the man a lesson. He

ran across the street as the woman started to get down. He gave her a hand, and when she was on the ground, she grabbed the side of the wagon and began to shake.

She pointed to the canvas-draped body. "The Halls done it. They shot him to death right in his office, and they made me cook their dinner."

Mark pulled the canvas away from the face of the dead man. He stood staring at it as if paralyzed. He was Jess Burke, all right. It was incredible that Jess, who had ruled Converse County so ruthlessly and so long, could have been murdered by the Halls.

Sharon had heard the commotion and had run out of the restaurant. Now she stood beside Mark, whispering, "My God, it's not possible."

The woman who had been in the wagon still stood there, both hands gripping the side of the wagon bed. "But it happened, Sharon. I was in the kitchen. When I heard the two shots, I ran into the office. Mr. Burke was lying on the floor dead and old man Hall threatened to shoot me if I didn't get back into the kitchen."

She began to tremble again, one hand coming up to her throat. She went on, her voice quivering. "I went back and cooked 'em a meal. All the time I was wishing for some arsenic or something, but I didn't even have any rat poison in the house."

"How many were there?" Mark asked.

"Six."

Sharon put an arm around the woman. "Come into my place, Bertha. You can rest there."

Sharon led her into the restaurant. A dozen men had gathered around the wagon. Each had his look at the dead man's face and then stepped back to form a loose circle. Now they stood in silence, awed, and probably thinking as Sharon had, that it wasn't possible.

Al Burke had heard the wagon thunder past the courthouse. Now he elbowed his way through the crowd and saw that it was his father in the wagon. He backed away just as the others had, staring at Jess's face that was hard set by death and seemed more ruthless than ever.

Slowly Burke raised his gaze to the man in the wagon seat. He asked, "What happened, Charlie?"

"The Halls done it," he man answered. "I didn't see it. Bertha can tell you about it. I didn't even know they were on the place until a couple of 'em walked into the cookshack. I was fixing some custard pies for supper. They threw a gun on me, made me sit down in a chair, and tied me. Later on they came back, untied me, and told me to get into the wagon and drive to town and tell you they'd be along purty soon and take the Dorn kid out of jail. Then they said they was gonna wipe the Burkes out before they got done."

"Where is Bertha?"

The man jerked his head toward Sharon's Beanery. "In there. Sharon took her."

"You take the body around to the back of the drugstore," Burke said. "You know where Doc Jones's undertaking parlor is. Some of you men go with him and help move the body. Ben," he nodded at the stableman, "you go tell Doc Jones what happened." He turned toward the restaurant, adding, "Stay here, Mark. I want to talk to Bertha."

Mark watched the wagon drive away, a few of the men following. The rest scattered, then gathered in small knots to talk about what had happened. In a strange way Mark was relieved. If Jess Burke had lived, Mark would have killed him sooner or later. He had known that from the first, and he had also known what it would do to Sharon and him.

Jess was dead, but by another man's hand, a man he had wronged just as he had wronged the Cardigans. Still Mark felt no great sense of satisfaction. He had kept hoping that Jess would change his mind and send some of his crew to help fight the Halls. Now, of course, there was no possibility of that. There wasn't time. The attack would probably come within the hour.

Burke returned, his face grave. "I guess it was bound to happen. When a man gets as bullheaded as pa and feels he's next to God, he just naturally brings it on himself. He was warned, but he wouldn't listen. I'm like Bertha, though. I never thought old man Hall would walk into the house like he owned it and smoke pa down."

"How do you feel?" Mark asked.

"Funny," Burke answered. "Like something was missing that ought to be here, like the sun ain't up there in the sky no more." He looked at Mark, then went on slowly, "How does anybody feel when the man who dominated him for so long is gone? I've hated him and I've loved him, I guess. He was the only parent I knew. He raised me. I owe him that, but God, he was stubborn. He told me I was old enough to blow my own nose, but he never would have forgiven me for doing it."

He stood there for a long moment chewing on his lower lip. Finally he said, "I'm glad of one thing, Mark. I broke with pa before this happened. I had a few hours of knowing he was alive, and still I was doing exactly what I goddamned pleased."

"It's up to you and Sharon now," Mark said.

Burke nodded. "I reckon it is."

"What are your plans?"

"We'll go to the courthouse and fight 'em off when they come after Bud Dorn," Burke said. "There's only six of 'em. I figgered there might be as many as ten. I told Sharon to fetch us some supper if they weren't here by six."

"You ever warn the townspeople?"

"No." Burke dragged the toe of his boot through the dust of the street. "I knew they might be some help and you got after me to do it, but I couldn't bring myself to scaring 'em to death over something I wasn't sure was going to happen. Now I guess it's too late. Anyhow, I think three of us can handle their six."

"There's only going to be two of you in the courthouse," Mark said.

Burke was startled, perhaps thinking, Mark told himself, that he was riding out of town and leaving the trouble in Burke's lap. But he didn't say it.

Instead he asked, "What do you mean by that?"

"I think I know outlaws better than you do," Mark said. "I had a few go-rounds with 'em in Baca County. It's my guess that old man Hall don't care either way about breaking Bud Dorn out of jail, though he may have meant what he said about wiping the Burkes out. The only thing the Halls are really interested in is money."

"I hadn't thought of it that way," Burke admitted. "We sure don't have much money in the courthouse."

"There's only one place in town that does have much money," Mark said.

Burke nodded. "The bank, and Uncle Rodney couldn't fight off a day-old pup."

"So I figure I'll stay in the bank, and you and Darby can hold the courthouse," Mark said.

"All right," Burke said reluctantly, "but you may wind up shooting it out with the whole kit and caboodle of 'em."

"I don't think so," Mark said. "I think they're more likely to split up."

"I hope so," Burke said and, turning, strode back toward the courthouse.

Mark watched him for a time, thinking about Sharon and Lucy, about Hall's threat to wipe the Burkes out which would include Sharon, and their intention of taking Lucy with them. He decided that their hunt for Lucy would be the last thing they'd do before they left town. He turned toward the bank, convinced it was the first place they'd hit.

CHAPTER XXV

Mark's first thought was to go into the bank and tell Rodney what was going to happen, then he remembered that neither Rodney nor his brother Bob had come into the street to learn what had happened. He also remembered that both of them had been with Jess Burke when his father and uncle were murdered. Maybe they had not been as responsible as Jess, but they had been there, had not raised a hand to stop the killings, and so they were at least partly to blame for what had happened.

He stood on the boardwalk in front of the bank, scratching the back of his neck, his gaze on the road to the north. He had come to Converse County to get rid of his nightmares. He had done that. He had wanted to learn the truth. He had done that. But now to risk his life to defend Rodney Burke's life and property was too much.

Still he had always been one to accept duty whatever it was. Aunt Kate had raised him that way, and he could not deny it now. He glanced at the star on his vest, ran a sleeve over it to remove a smudged fingerprint, and shook his head. He had no choice, but he would not go inside and tell Rodney what to expect and then sit down and wait for the Halls.

It was only fair for Rodney to face the Halls, to know that death was barely a finger twitch on a trigger from him. But more to the point Mark would have a greater advantage if the Halls didn't know he was there. He remembered what Al Burke had said about shooting it out with the whole kit and caboodle of them. If he had to swap lead with six outlaws, he needed all the advantage he could get.

He walked along the side of the bank, remembering there was a back door and a hall that led along the side of Rodney's office into the bank proper. He wasn't sure whether the back door was kept locked or not. If it was, he'd have to rethink his course of action. He rounded the corner of the building, reached the door, and tried the knob. He was lucky. The door opened, and he slipped inside and closed the door behind him.

The door at the other end of the hall was shut, so he found himself in absolute darkness. He'd had a view of the hall before he'd closed the back door and had seen that it was clear, so he walked slowly along it, his hands outstretched in front of him. When his fingertips touched the door, he ran one hand downward along the edge until he found the knob. He turned it and pushed the door open a crack.

He could not see all the bank, but he could see the safe and the teller's desk. Apparently the teller was also the bookkeeper because he was sitting at his desk working on what Mark guessed was a ledger. Probably Bob had nothing to do except sit at his desk and nap and smoke cigars, stirred into movement only when someone came in for a loan.

Mark settled down to wait, but he discovered he

was more nervous than he had realized. He drew the makings from his pocket and rolled a cigarette, then decided the smell of tobacco smoke would give his presence away to the teller, so he tossed the cigarette to the floor.

The minutes dragged by. He watched the teller get up and go into the office, then return and sit down and pick up his pen. He could not see the clock on the wall, so he had no way of judging time, but it seemed to him that hours had passed before he saw the teller sit back and put his pen down, his face suddenly turning ashen. Someone or more than one had just come in.

Mark heard spurs jingle as two men crossed the front of the bank and came into view. Both held guns, but it was the old one who gave the orders. He jerked his left hand savagely at the teller as he said, "I want to see Rodney Burke about a withdrawal. Get him."

The teller jumped up and scurried toward the office. He returned a moment later, Rodney waddling behind him. Rodney started to bluster, then he stopped, his face turning pale. He said in a shrill, frightened tone, "By God, you're Hall, ain't you?"

Old man Hall shook his left fist in Rodney's face. "You're damned right I'm Hall. I've come to collect what you have been owing me for a long time. I've killed Jess and I'm going to kill you. Right now you're going to open the safe and put the money in this sack." He jerked his head at the younger man. "Hand it to him, Rafe."

The other man held out the sack. "Fill it up," he said.

Rodney didn't move. Mark wasn't sure whether he was paralyzed or simply playing for time, but the old man was not in a mood to wait. He fired a shot at Rodney's feet. "It's up to you how you die. Slow by me shooting off your fingers and then your ears and finally your nose, or do I put a slug into your brisket?"

Mark shoved the door open wide enough to slip through and edged into the bank. Rodney was moving like a man sleepwalking. He took the sack and approached the safe. He got down on his knees and started working on it. Just as he finished opening the safe, Mark ordered, "Hook the moon, Hall. Both of you."

For a very small interval of time neither Hall moved, then they wheeled, both firing. Mark, expecting this, was ready. He pulled the trigger on his gun with the first move the old man made. Both of the Halls' shots were wild, but Mark's first slug ripped through the side of the old man's head.

Mark dropped to the floor the instant after he pulled the trigger, rolled, and fired two more times. Young Hall was staggered by the first slug, the second was a complete miss, but the first shot had smashed his right arm. He dropped the gun and stooped to pick it up with his left hand.

Mark, on his feet now, said, "Don't do it, mister. You're dead if you do."

Hall straightened, his left hand moving up to touch his shattered right arm. "You broke it," he said accusingly. "You son of a bitch, you broke it."

Mark picked up both guns and pressed them into Rodney's hands, but Rodney couldn't make his hands function well enough to grip them. He was shaking as if he had a chill; his face had turned to a ghastly yellow-green. He apparently heard what Mark said because he tried to raise both arms, but they fell back after coming halfway up.

"He was going to kill me," Rodney whispered as if he still found it hard to believe. "He was really going to kill me."

Mark heard shooting from the courthouse. He turned to the teller. "I've got to give Al a hand. You take the guns and hold one of 'em on Hall. If he bats an eye, kill him."

The teller wasn't much better off than Rodney, but he took the guns, laid one on the desk and, cocking the other one, lined it on the wounded man. Mark left the bank on the run. He had no idea how long the shooting had been going on, but he didn't think it was much longer than it had taken him to handle the old man and his son in the bank. It had stopped now, and that, he thought, might not be a good sign.

He ran up the middle of the street. When he reached the corner of the block that held the courthouse, two men rode around the building from the back and headed directly toward him, cracking steel to their horses on every jump. Both were bent over their saddle horns as if badly hurt. Mark realized only then that he had not taken time to reload, that he had used three shells in the bank.

"Pull up," Mark yelled.

Either they didn't hear or decided to make a run for it. They kept coming, riding hard, directly at him. He fired at the one on his left and knocked him out of the saddle. He missed the second shot, but the remaining man had had enough. He reined his horse to a stop and sat weaving in the saddle, one hand pressed against his right shoulder, blood oozing between his fingers.

A few seconds later Al Burke and Luke Darby came racing out of the courthouse. Burke wasn't hurt, but Darby had a stream of blood running down his forehead.

"What about the bank?" Darby demanded when he reached Mark.

"The old man's dead and the one with him is wounded," Mark answered. "The teller's holding him."

Burke wheeled to face Darby. "Get the doc to tie up your head, then send him over here. Mark, help me get this jasper off his saddle and into jail."

Later, when the wounded men had been locked up and the bodies of the dead men moved to Doc Jones's undertaking room, Burke had time to tell Mark what had happened.

"The Dorns came in through the front door shooting," Burke said. "They acted like they were crazy. We gunned 'em down, and it wasn't until then that the two Halls who were outside our office window started shooting. They should have plugged both of us, but the best they could do was to give Darby a scalping. We hit both of 'em, and they took out of there.

"We heard the shooting from the bank right then, and I suppose that upset them. I guess there wasn't supposed to be any trouble there. Rafe told me the old man had been scheming on his plan all the time he was in the canyon, and he figured it would go off without a hitch. In fact, Rafe was surprised that you had figured it out. He thought we'd all be in the courthouse."

Burke slapped Mark on the shoulder. "I've got to hand it to you, Deputy. If it had been me, we would all have been in the courthouse."

"Don't hand me anything," Mark said. "I might have outsmarted myself if more of them had come into the bank." He shook his head. "You know, Al, now that it's over, I'm mighty weak in the knees."

"So am I," Burke said. "What are you going to do, Mark? I have a notion you were staying on here mostly to help me out of a jam."

"I was," Mark admitted. "I dunno what I'll do. Head back to Baca County, I guess. I've done what I came for."

"Before you start, let's go see Rodney," Burke said.

"I don't have any hankering to see . . ." Mark began.

"Come on." Burke grabbed his arm. "I just saw Sharon go into the bank. You wouldn't leave without telling her good-bye?"

"No, I ain't in that much of a hurry," Mark said.

The smell of burnt gunpowder still lingered in the bank when Mark and Burke went in. The teller was sitting at his desk. That was all he was doing. Just sitting, and from the expression on his face, Mark thought that was all he was capable of doing.

Rodney Burke was in the same condition. His face had lost its yellow-green tinge, but he was still trembling. He was sweating and he appeared to be completely worn out.

Sharon smiled when she saw Mark. She said, "I guess it was a lucky day for us when you rode into town."

"Sharon," Al said, "this ugly galoot is talking about going back to Baca County."

"You can't do that, Mark." Sharon took his hand. "I guess you have an idea, after the way your father and uncle were treated, that there is no place for you in

Converse County. I'm not apologizing for my father. None of us can overlook what he did."

She paused for a moment, then added thoughtfully, "It's hard to even say I loved him, but I did in a qualified sort of way. Of course I didn't know him at the time he killed your father. At least I don't remember what he was like then, but I'm sure he mellowed over the years. I can remember moments when he showed Al and me some tenderness, but there weren't many of them. I guess I both loved and hated him."

"I told Mark that was the way I felt," Al said. "It's the only way we could have felt."

Sharon nodded agreement, then said, "Anyhow, Mark, we need you here in East Park. I need you in particular, so Al and I had a talk. Uncle Rodney tells me that Al and I are the sole heirs to pa's estate. We have agreed to deed Cardigan valley to you. It's only right."

"It wouldn't work," Mark said. "I don't have the money to stock a ranch."

"Uncle Rodney has an idea about that," Sharon said, "especially since you just saved his life."

Rodney cleared his throat. He said, "The bank will loan you all you need and you can pick your own time to repay it."

"Or maybe never," Al suggested.

Rodney choked. He wiped his face with a white handkerchief. With an effort he said, "Or never."

"See how cheerful he is about helping you?" Sharon said. "You can't turn down an offer like that."

Mark looked at Rodney, a pitiful fat man who had more the appearance of a fat toad than a human being. Suddenly he realized he did not hate the man. Rodney Burke was not worth hating.

"Now that I think about it," Mark said, "I guess there is nothing in Baca County that I have to go back to."

He looked at Sharon who was standing very close to him. It was plain that she expected to be kissed, so he kissed her.

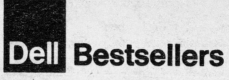

DELL'S ACTION-PACKED WESTERNS

Selected Titles

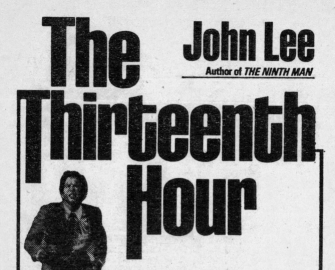

The Thirteenth Hour

John Lee

Author of *THE NINTH MAN*

Pursued by the SS, threatened by the Russian advance, Captain Henry Bascom has only cunning and sheer luck on his side. But when he becomes the sole witness to an incredible Nazi plot to save Hitler, he knows he will need more than cunning and luck to survive!

A Dell Book $2.50   (18751-6)